S0-AYS-066

He'd waited ten years for this....

When he'd last made love to Marie she'd been a girl. Now the naked body before him was that of a woman. And she kissed like she had in his dreams. She was so precious to him, so perfect. He wanted to hold her forever, never wanted to lose her.

To lose her....

He pushed the morose thought away, trying to be happy for once in his life. But he knew he wouldn't be, not if something happened to Marie. Not if he lost her. In his arms he had everything he wanted—right here, right now— yet he was more conscious than ever of how quickly it all could be taken away. How quickly Marie could be taken away.

In his mind, the eerie voice spoke again. *All that you love will die....*

ANN VOSS PETERSON

CHRISTMAS AWAKENING

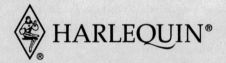

HARLEQUIN®

TORONTO • NEW YORK • LONDON
AMSTERDAM • PARIS • SYDNEY • HAMBURG
STOCKHOLM • ATHENS • TOKYO • MILAN • MADRID
PRAGUE • WARSAW • BUDAPEST • AUCKLAND

If you purchased this book without a cover you should be aware
that this book is stolen property. It was reported as "unsold and
destroyed" to the publisher, and neither the author nor the
publisher has received any payment for this "stripped book."

To Rebecca, Norman and Patricia and our wonderful
time exploring Maryland's eastern shore.

Recycling programs
for this product may
not exist in your area.

ISBN-13: 978-0-373-69362-7
ISBN-10:   0-373-69362-1

CHRISTMAS AWAKENING

Copyright © 2008 by Ann Voss Peterson

All rights reserved. Except for use in any review, the reproduction or
utilization of this work in whole or in part in any form by any electronic,
mechanical or other means, now known or hereafter invented, including
xerography, photocopying and recording, or in any information storage
or retrieval system, is forbidden without the written permission of the
publisher, Harlequin Enterprises Limited, 225 Duncan Mill Road,
Don Mills, Ontario, Canada M3B 3K9.

This is a work of fiction. Names, characters, places and incidents are
either the product of the author's imagination or are used fictitiously,
and any resemblance to actual persons, living or dead, business
establishments, events or locales is entirely coincidental.

This edition published by arrangement with Harlequin Books S.A.

® and TM are trademarks of the publisher. Trademarks indicated with
® are registered in the United States Patent and Trademark Office, the
Canadian Trade Marks Office and in other countries.

www.eHarlequin.com

Printed in U.S.A.

ABOUT THE AUTHOR

Ever since she was a little girl making her own books out of construction paper, Ann Voss Peterson wanted to write. So when it came time to choose a major at the University of Wisconsin, creative writing was her only choice. Of course, writing wasn't a *practical* choice—one needs to earn a living. So Ann found jobs ranging from proofreading legal transcripts to working with quarter horses to washing windows. But no matter how she earned her paycheck, she continued to write the type of stories that captured her heart and imagination—romantic suspense. Ann lives near Madison, Wisconsin, with her husband, her two young sons, her border collie and her quarter horse mare. Ann loves to hear from readers. E-mail her at ann@annvosspeterson.com or visit her Web site at www.annvosspeterson.com.

Books by Ann Voss Peterson

CAST OF CHARACTERS

Marie Leonard—The butler's daughter, Marie returned to Jenkins Cove to bury her father and bring his murderer to justice.

Brandon Drake—After his wife died in a fiery car crash, he became a recluse. Was it due to grief…or guilt?

Charlotte Drake—The beautiful and accomplished lady of Drake House had everything, except the one thing she wanted most.

Edwin Leonard—The butler of Drake House died under suspicious circumstances.

Aunt Sophie Caldwell—A batty old woman who believes in psychic phenomena.

Police Chief Charles Hammer—Is the police chief of Jenkins Cove lazy or hiding something?

Ned Perry—Would he kill to get his hands on prime real estate?

Clifford Drake—How far will he go to get his hands on Drake House?

Phil Cardon—A young man who does odd jobs in town.

Josef Novak—The chauffeur came to America to find his fortune. But when he tried to bring his betrothed wife over, his dream went horribly wrong.

Shelley Zachary—After Edwin's death, Shelley took over running Drake House, and she loves the power. How far will she go to keep it?

Isabella Faust—How far will she go to wear Brandon's or Cliff's ring?

Doug Heller—The manager of Drake Enterprises seems to have his eye on, and hand in, everything going on in Jenkins Cove.

Prologue

Edwin Leonard's heart beat hard enough to break a rib. He adjusted his reading glasses and studied the sketch's deft lines. So much detail. So much planning.

This was proof. Proof of murder.

He slipped his glasses into his pocket. He'd been butler at Drake House since he was a young man, yet he never would have guessed such hatred pulsed within the borders of his beloved estate. Such a malicious, *murderous* force. The paper rattled in his shaking hand, fear adding to the tremor he'd acquired with age.

He needed to hide the sketch. Stash it away until he could get it to the police. If the killer found it and destroyed it, the only evidence of murder would be Edwin's word.

And that of a ghost.

He circled Drake House's south wing and followed the freshly laid oyster shell path through the south garden. The soles of his shoes crunched with each step. Too loud.

He paused, scanning the area, making sure no one had heard. The old mansion's grounds were quiet; only the lap of waves on rock along the shoreline reached him. He was alone. Even so, he found himself holding his breath.

Stepping along the edge of the path, he continued. He had to stash the sketch and get back into the house before anyone noticed his absence. He knew just the hiding place. A spot where no one would think to look.

He quickened his pace, following the white shells into the redesigned east garden. He stopped at a bench nestled among holly bushes and grasped the seat. Grunting with effort, he shifted the seat to the side, exposing a hollow space in the concrete base.

A space just the right size.

He rolled the sketch in trembling hands and slipped it into the crevice. He shifted the seat back into place.

It would be safe there. Safe until morning when he could turn it over to Police Chief Hammer. Still, something didn't feel right. Maybe it was nerves. Maybe it was some sort of sixth sense. Maybe it was related to what he'd experienced in the candlelit room in Sophie's attic. Whatever caused the feeling, it bore down on him, thicker and more invasive than the humid, late autumn night.

Anger. Evil.

He had to get a hold of himself. Straightening, he combed his hair into place with his fingers. He brushed off his suit, pulled a linen handkerchief from his pocket and dried his palms. Extracting his timepiece from his pocket, he tilted the face to catch the light of the moon.

Mr. Brandon would wonder what had happened to him if his bed wasn't turned down when he chose to retire. That certainly wouldn't do.

Edwin slipped the watch back into his vest pocket. It clinked against the skeleton key he'd stolen along with the sketch.

The key. He'd forgotten to stash the key. Turning back toward the bench, he reached into his pocket.

The blow hit him before he could react. The force shuddered through his skull and down his spine. He dropped to his knees on the sharp shells.

Another blow brought darkness. He couldn't move. He couldn't think. He felt his legs being lifted, his body being dragged down the path. Out of the garden. Over the lawn. To the pier jutting out into the bay.

No. Not the water.

He tried to move, to fight, but his body wouldn't obey. Rough hands pushed him. He rolled into the water. Salt filled his mouth. Cold lapped at his body. His head went under.

Then he felt nothing.

Chapter One

"When a loved one dies, it's normal to want answers, Miss Leonard," the police chief drawled. He stopped near the break in the boxwood hedge that opened to the Jenkins Cove Chapel's redbrick walkway, as if he couldn't wait to get out of the graveyard…or maybe just away from Marie. "But sometimes you got to accept that accidents happen."

Accept? Marie gripped a damp tissue in her fist. Maybe she could accept, *if* her father's death really *was* an accident.

She focused on the arrangement of holly and poinsettia draping Edwin Leonard's casket. It was all wrong. The sunny day and cheery Christmas greenery. The sparsity of the black-clad crowd that wandered away from the graveside now that they'd offered their condolences. And most of all, the words coming from the chief's mouth. "I know you've ruled my father's death an accident, Chief Hammer. I'd like to know what led you to that conclusion."

"What led me?" The police chief drew up to his full height, what little there was of it.

A squat, bulldog of a man, Charles Hammer had

struck Marie as lazy, ever since he'd poo-pooed her report of boys smoking marijuana back when she was a sophomore at Jenkins Cove High. His quickness to dismiss her father's death as an accident before he knew all the circumstances just underscored that impression. Obviously nothing had changed in the ten years since she'd left Maryland's Eastern Shore. "Why do you think it was an accident?"

His mouth curved into a patronizing smile. "The evidence of accidental death is pretty clear in your father's case. In fact, nothing suggests it was anything *but* an accident. He was walking on the dock at night. He slipped and hit his head on the rocks along the shoreline. Accidental drowning. Pure and simple."

"It couldn't have happened that way."

"I know." He shook his head slowly, his bald scalp catching the sun's rays. "It seems so random."

Tension radiated up Marie's neck, fueling the headache that throbbed behind her eyes. "No, that's not it. It couldn't have happened the way you said. It's not possible."

He peered down his pudgy nose. "That's what our evidence indicates."

"The evidence is wrong."

"Evidence is never wrong."

"Then the way you're looking at it is wrong."

He drew in his chin, making himself look like an offended old lady. Or a turtle. "What do you do for a living, Miss Leonard?"

"I'm a philosophy professor."

He grinned as if that explained everything. "Well, I'm a police chief. I deal in hard evidence, not silly theories. I've investigated deaths before. Have you?"

She let out a frustrated breath. Her father had always warned her about her lack of tact. She should have tiptoed around the chief's ego. Flattered him. Buttered him up. Then he would probably be more open to her ideas. Instead, she'd turned him into an enemy.

She stared up at the spire of the gray stone church she'd attended as a kid. "I'm sorry. There's just something you don't understand."

"I understand the evidence. And in your father's case, that evidence clearly says accidental drowning."

She leveled her gaze back on the chief. "That's what I'm trying to tell you. My father never would have accidentally drowned."

"Your father hit his head. Even Olympic champions can't swim when they're unconscious."

"My father couldn't swim. Not a stroke."

"Then how can you find accidental drowning impossible?"

She tried to swallow the thickness in her throat.

"Because he was deathly afraid of the water. He never would have gone near it."

The chief looked unimpressed. He edged closer to the redbrick path between the boxwood. "I'm sorry, Miss Leonard. Facts are facts. Your father did go near the water that night. The case is closed. I'm sorry for your loss."

The finality of his words struck her like a kick to the sternum. She watched him amble down the path and join the last of the funeral-goers milling along Main Street.

The man from the funeral parlor eyed her from beside her father's casket, waiting for her to leave so he could lower Edwin Leonard to his final resting place beside her mother.

Marie pulled the collar of her black wool coat tighter around her shoulders. She didn't know if murder victims truly rested or not, but she sure wouldn't. Not until she knew what had happened to her father.

Not until she made his killer pay.

MARIE FORCED HER FEET to move up the loose gravel walk to the kitchen entrance of the sprawling white antebellum mansion. Drake House. An uneasy feeling pinched the back of her neck. The feeling she was being watched.

She spun around, searching the grounds. Waves danced on Chesapeake Bay and the mouth of Jenkins Creek, a body of water ironically broader and deeper than many lakes. Evening shadow cloaked the mansion's facade, transforming it to a dark hulk against the gleam of sunset on water. It looked austere, empty. The Christmas decorations that blanketed every house and shop in town were nowhere to be found here. No evergreen swags draping the balconies. No wreaths adorning the doors. Dark windows stared down at her like probing eyes.

She was home.

A bitter laugh died in her throat. She might have grown up in this house, but it wasn't home. Not without her father.

A gust of wind blew off the water, tangling her funeral-black skirt around her legs. Even though it was early December, the wind felt warm to Marie. And the shiver that ran over her skin had nothing to do with temperature.

Was someone watching her from the house? Brandon? A flutter moved through her stomach. She gritted her teeth against the sensation. The last time she'd seen Brandon Drake, she'd been a teenager with delusions of true love. She'd changed a lot since then. Grown stronger. Wiser. Her heart had shattered and mended. Still, she'd been relieved when Brandon Drake hadn't attended her father's service. She didn't want to see him. Not when she was aching from her father's loss. Not when her emotions were so raw. Not when she was feeling less than strong.

Unfortunately, if she wanted to find the truth about her father's murder, she had to start at the place he'd lived…and died. Drake House.

She tore her gaze from the mansion's upper floors and the balcony that ran the length of the private wing. Setting her chin, she increased her pace. The quicker she could get into her father's quarters, look through his things and get out, the better. It was all over town that Brandon had become a recluse since his wife died. He didn't take visitors. If she entered through the kitchen and dealt with the servants, maybe she could find enough to convince Chief Hammer to reopen her father's case as a homicide without ever having to face Brandon Drake.

At least she could hope.

Unease tickled over her again, raising the hair on her arms. She looked up at the house, beyond to the boat-house, then turned toward the carriage house. A man with the flat and misshapen nose of a prizefighter stared at her from the other side of a long black car. He nodded a greeting, then resumed rubbing the hood with a chamois.

The chauffeur. She recognized him from her father's funeral. At least someone from Drake House had come.

She gave the chauffeur a little wave, circled a gray

stone wall surrounding the pool and clomped up the wooden steps. Pressing the doorbell, she peered through wavy glass and into the kitchen where she'd once had milk and cookies after school.

It looked so much the same. Too much the same. A dull ache throbbed in her chest.

A woman with the thin, strong look of steel wire bustled across the kitchen and opened the door. Penciled eyebrows tilted over curious eyes. "Yes?"

"I'm Marie Leonard."

"Of course. Miss Leonard. I'm so sorry about your father." She opened the door with one hand, using the other to usher Marie inside. "I'm Shelley. Shelley Zachary. We talked on the phone."

Marie nodded. The cook, now housekeeper. The woman Brandon Drake had promoted to take over her father's job before he was even in the ground.

"It's nice to finally meet you. I worked side by side with Edwin for the past eight years, and a day didn't go by that he didn't mention you. I'm so sorry I wasn't able to make it to his funeral. Running a house like this in addition to cooking is very demanding."

Marie forced a smile she didn't feel. "I'm here to go through my father's things."

"Of course. Isabella can help you, if you need it."

Marie followed the housekeeper's gaze to the corner of the kitchen where a young woman with huge blue eyes and luxurious, auburn hair polished a silver tea service. She wore a uniform of black slacks and blouse with a white apron, more covered than the stereotypical French maid, yet because of her bombshell body, nearly as sexy.

"Isabella? This is Edwin's daughter."

Isabella continued with her work as if she couldn't care less.

At one time, the servants at Drake House were Marie's family, and a caring and tightly knit one at that. Not just her father, but everyone who'd worked at the house back then, from the maid to the cook to the chauffeur, liked to read her stories and bring her treats. They watched out for her, and she never questioned that each cared about her and about each other.

Clearly that family atmosphere had deserted Drake House in the past ten years.

That was fine. Marie didn't need a surrogate family. She needed answers. She focused on Shelley Zachary. "Do you have my father's keys?"

"Of course. I'm running the house now."

"May I have them? Or at least the keys to his quarters?"

"You don't need keys. Isabella can assist you."

Marie pressed her lips together. She didn't want someone looking over her shoulder. "I can handle it myself."

"You'll need help. Your father lived here a long time. Cleaning out his quarters is going to be a big job."

She was sure it would be. Especially since she intended to do a little snooping while she was here. "Really, I'd rather be alone. You understand."

Shelley Zachary didn't look as though she understood at all, but she nodded all the same. "Fine. But before I give you keys, I'll have to clear it with Mr. Brandon."

The name zapped along Marie's nerves like an electric charge. "No, that's not necessary."

Shelley frowned. "Excuse me? He's the master of the

house. He certainly has a say in who can and cannot have keys to his property."

There she went again, speaking without thinking, making enemies where a little tact might have made her an ally. Marie held up her hands, palms out. "That's not what I meant. It's just that I know he's busy. And I hear he's not taking many visitors lately."

The severe line to Shelley's mouth softened slightly. "No, he's not. Not since he lost his Charlotte."

A pang registered in Marie's chest at the sound of Brandon's wife's name…even after all these years.

"He never minds a visit from me." Isabella tossed Marie a smug smile. "I'll ask him."

"Ask me what?"

Marie's heart stuttered. She looked to the dark doorway leading to the dining room for the source of the deep voice.

Brandon Drake emerged from the dining room shadow. His shoulders filled the doorway. The dying rays of the sun streamed sideways from the kitchen windows and fell on his face.

Marie gasped.

A scar ran from his temple to the corner of his mouth, slick, red skin slashing across his cheek. He stepped forward, leaning on a brass and teak cane. "Hello, Marie."

Chapter Two

Brandon could see Marie stifle a gasp as she took in his face, his limp. The thought of her seeing his weakness hurt more than the burns themselves. He tore his eyes from her, not wanting to witness more, and focused on Isabella. "What were you going to ask me?"

The little vixen didn't answer. Instead, Shelley piped up. "Miss Leonard is here to clear out her father's things. She asked for keys to the butler's quarters."

"Give her the keys."

"You're hurt." Marie's voice was almost a whisper, as if she was murmuring her thoughts aloud, not intending for the rest of them to hear.

He kept his gaze on Shelley, careful not to look in Marie's direction. Her hair was a little shorter than it had been ten years ago, only jaw length now, and her face had lost its teenage roundness. But she was still Marie. He couldn't take seeing horror on her face as she scrutinized his injuries. Or worse, pity. "Where are those keys, Shelley?"

"I'll get them, sir." Shelley bustled off into the pantry.

Marie stepped toward him. She raised her hand.

Brandon wasn't sure what she intended to do. Touch

him? Soothe him? Heal him? He stepped back, removing himself from her reach. "It's nothing, Marie. I'm fine. Charlotte was the one who was hurt."

Pink suffused Marie's cheeks. She dropped her hand to her side and clutched a fistful of her black skirt. "I know. I mean, I'm sorry about your wife's death."

Guilt dug into his gut. He was such an ass. Sure he had to keep his distance from Marie. He owed Edwin that much. Just as he owed Charlotte. And when it came right down to it, he owed Marie. But he could have kept away from her without slapping her down. Just one more bit of proof that he didn't belong anywhere near someone as decent as Marie Leonard.

"My father didn't tell me you were hurt as well."

"Like I said, it's nothing." He glanced at the pantry. Where was Shelley with those keys?

"It's not nothing. If I'd known, I would have come...I would have—" She let her words hang as if she suddenly recognized the inappropriateness of what she was saying. She dipped her chin, looking down at his hand gripping the cane, at the wedding ring still on his finger. "Anyway, I'm sorry."

He nodded, hoping she was finished. "You don't have to put yourself through all this, Marie. Isabella can pack up Edwin's things and send them to you."

"No. I want to do it myself. It will...it will make me feel closer to him."

Brandon gripped the head of his cane until his fingers ached. The thought of Marie spending time in Drake House threatened to unhinge him. Even two floors up and in another wing, he'd be aware of every move she made. But what could he say? That she couldn't pack her father's things? That he refused to let her into the house where she'd grown up? That would make him more of an SOB than he already was. He forced his head to bob in a nod. "Take all the time you need."

"Thanks. You won't even know I'm here."

Fat chance of that.

Silence stretched between them, each second feeling like a minute. From outside he heard waves slap the shore and a yacht hum on Jenkins Creek, probably his uncle taking advantage of the unusually warm December.

Weather. That would get his mind off Marie. Sure. Where in the hell was Shelley?

Brandon cleared his throat. "I'm sorry about Edwin. He was a good man. I don't know what I'm going to do without him."

Tears glistened in Marie's eyes, but they didn't fall. "Thank you."

A car door slammed outside.

Isabella looked up from the tea service she was buffing.

Brandon held up a hand. "I'll get it." He headed for the kitchen door, trying not to lean too heavily on his cane. He was sure the maid was wondering what was going on. Since Charlotte died, he'd refused visitors whenever possible. But right now he had to get out of the cramped kitchen. He had to get away from Marie.

How on earth was he going to handle having her in his house the next few days?

IN THE PAST TEN YEARS, Marie had imagined countless times what it might be like to see Brandon again. But even in her worst nightmares, she'd never pictured things going so badly.

"All right. Here you go." Shelley Zachary emerged from the pantry with a set of keys jangling in her hand. "There's a key for this kitchen door and one for the butler suite. That should be all you need."

Marie nodded. She was hoping for her father's set, which held keys for everything on the estate, just in case she needed to follow up on anything she found. But she didn't see how she could ask for that without raising more than a few eyebrows. She'd just have to figure out another way to snoop. "Thank you."

"Where is Mr. Brandon?"

"Talking to Doug Heller." A tray with the tea service in her hands, Isabella nodded in the direction of the kitchen door, then disappeared through the arched hall to the dining room.

Marie peered through the windows to the porch. His back to her, Brandon was talking to a man dressed in jeans, work boots and a rough canvas coat. The name sounded familiar to her, as if her father might have mentioned it at some point. "Who is Doug Heller?"

As if sensing her scrutiny, the man talking to Brandon raised his weather-beaten face and stared at her through watery blue eyes.

A chill raced over her skin.

Shelley crossed the kitchen. "He works for Drake Enterprises. Operations manager."

"I thought Brandon was running the foundation. Is he back working for the company?"

Shelley plopped the keys into Marie's hand. "No, no. Brandon's uncle is still running Drake Enterprises. Mr. Brandon has his hands full with the foundation."

"Then why is the operations manager here?"

"Oh, I'm betting he's not here about Drake Enterprises. It's probably about that developer again. Ned Perry. He's trying to buy up waterfront property. More tenacious than a terrier."

"Developer? Brandon isn't thinking of…" She couldn't finish. The thought was too abhorrent.

"Selling Drake House? Turning it into condos?" Shelley laughed. "Mr. Brandon would rather die."

A morbid thought, but one that inspired relief. At least he still loved the historic old mansion. And though it might not feel like home without her father here, Marie had to admit being inside these walls made her feel grounded for the first time since Chief Hammer had called to break the news of her father's death. "I'm glad to hear he's not selling. It's just when I saw no Christmas decorations and then you mentioned a developer…"

"Mr. Brandon has canceled the Christmas Ball, I'm afraid."

Marie frowned. The annual Christmas Ball and charity auction was an institution in Jenkins Cove. "That's too bad."

"He said there's no point without Charlotte here. Oh, and your father. He doesn't even feel like celebrating Christmas."

"I'm sorry to hear that." Marie was. Brandon had always embraced Christmas, especially since the annual ball and auction brought in a lot of money the foundation could distribute to people in need. Brandon had always believed in spreading his good fortune to others. It was the reason he'd devoted his life to the foundation instead of taking his spot at the head of his family's company. It was one of the many things she'd admired about him.

Marie shook her head. She couldn't afford to nurse good feelings about Brandon and Drake House. Not unless she wanted to forget herself the way she had when she'd first seen his scarred face. She had to remember things were different than they were the summer before she'd gone to college. And even then, things between her and Brandon weren't really the way she'd imagined them to be.

Marie let out a heavy sigh. Her father had always said the old-money Drakes were different from working people. That even though she grew up in Drake House, she didn't belong in their world. That summer after high school graduation, when Brandon had given his mother's diamond ring to Charlotte instead of her, she'd finally realized her father was right.

"…to Sophie Caldwell."

Marie snapped her attention back to Shelley. "I'm sorry. What did you say?"

The woman blew a derisive breath through her nose. "I said, you should talk to Sophie Caldwell."

It took a second for her to process the name. "The woman who runs the bed-and-breakfast down by the harbor?"

Shelley nodded. "The House of the Seven Gables. Word was Sophie and Edwin were quite the item."

Her father? Seeing a woman? "He never said anything to me."

"That might not be something a father tells a daughter."

Marie didn't appreciate the woman's gossipy tone, but this time she managed to hold her tongue. As unlikable as she found Shelley Zachary, the woman was the best source of information she had when it came to her father and the goings-on at Drake House. "I wish he'd told me. I always worried he'd been lonely."

"He didn't have time to be lonely. Just ask Josef."

"Josef?"

"Our chauffeur. Josef Novak. Poor Josef. Another man who lost his love. She died in the hospital. An illness, just like the way your mother went. He used to drive Edwin to the Seven Gables several times a week. He doesn't talk much, but he probably understood your father better than anyone, except Sophie, of course."

Of course. Marie pictured the man who'd been buffing the car outside, the man who'd waved to her and had attended her father's funeral. Josef. She couldn't imagine her father having many heart-to-hearts with the quiet chauffeur, no matter how much they had in common. Better to go straight to the source, Sophie Caldwell.

She glanced at Brandon through the kitchen windows. The manager, Doug Heller, was still stealing glances at her that gave her the creeps, but judging from the men's body language, their conversation was drawing to a close.

And that meant Brandon would be returning to the kitchen.

"I think I'll run over to talk to Sophie Caldwell right now. Will you pass my thanks to Brandon for the keys? I'm parked out front, so I'll just scurry out through the foyer."

"Fine." Shelley looked pleased to be rid of her. Maybe that was her intent all along.

"I'll be back later tonight to start on my father's things."

"Fine. Don't park near the kitchen. This is a busy house."

Late at night? Marie doubted it, but miraculously held her tongue. The decision to leave and come back later was looking better all the time. Later, after the servants were gone. And after Brandon had retired to his third-floor suite.

When she could be alone.

Chapter Three

It didn't take long for Marie to drive into the town of Jenkins Cove and wind her way through its quaint little streets. She parked in a lot off Royal Oak Street and walked the rest of the way to the bed-and-breakfast.

Connected to the harbor area by a narrow, concrete bridge, the House of the Seven Gables perched on the edge of the water. Masts of sailboats jutted into the twilight sky. A few yachts docked at a seafood restaurant nearby, and the scent of crab cakes teased the air. Christmas music mixed with the lap of the waves.

Unlike Drake House, the bed-and-breakfast was already decked out for the season. Wreaths adorned every door. Ropes of holly wrapped the porch posts and draped the balcony above. Marie climbed the steps to the front and rang the bell.

Footfalls approached, creaking across a wood floor. The door swung inward and a pleasantly plump, gray-haired woman peered out. A broad smile stretched across her Cupid's bow lips and crinkled the corners of her eyes. "Merry Christmas. Please, come in." She wiped her hands on her apron and gestured Marie inside with a sweep of her arm.

Marie couldn't help but return the woman's smile. She looked familiar, and Marie was fairly certain she'd seen her at the funeral.

"Are you interested in a room? We have one left overlooking the harbor."

"No, thanks." Was this the woman her father had been seeing? She hoped so. The woman seemed so gregarious and kind. Marie would like to think her father had someone like this caring about him and sharing his life in his final months. "I'm Marie Leonard."

"Of course. Edwin's daughter. I'm sorry I didn't recognize you right away." She opened her arms and engulfed Marie in a soft hug. When she finally released her grip, the woman had tears in her eyes. "I'm so happy to meet you, dear. I wanted to talk to you at your father's funeral today, but I…" She fanned her face, unable to go on.

A stinging sensation burned the back of Marie's eyes. She blinked. Getting her emotions under control, she met the woman's blue gaze. "I need to ask you some questions about my father, Ms…"

"Sophie. Please, call me Sophie." She took Marie's coat and led her into a parlor with windows gazing out onto the garden and the water beyond. She gestured to the corner of the room where an easel propped up an artist's canvas. The scent of paint thinner tinged the air. "And this is my niece, Chelsea."

Marie started. She hadn't even noticed someone else was in the room. She looked beyond the canvas and into the beautifully haunting face of a blue-eyed blonde. "Nice to meet you."

The young woman nodded. Quietly, she set down her paintbrush and glanced out the window as if her thoughts were far away.

Marie couldn't put her finger on it, but there was something about her…something disconcerting. As if when Chelsea looked out over the water, she could see things Marie couldn't even imagine.

Sophie ushered her to a grouping of white wicker near the canvas. "Please, sit down and feel free to ask me whatever is on your mind, honey."

Marie lowered herself into a chair across from Sophie. Staring at the cameo necklace around Sophie's neck, Marie searched for the right words to lead into her questions. "About my father…you two were close?"

The woman nodded her gray head. "Your father was a light in my life." Again, her eyes filled with tears.

Marie fought her own surge of emotion. Silence filled the room, making her feel the need to break it. She wanted to ask if Sophie knew who would murder her father, but how was she supposed to do that? The woman was obviously as grief-stricken as she herself. Throwing around suspicions of murder might send Sophie over the edge. Tact. Marie needed to use some sort of tact. To tread carefully for once in her life. "How did the two of you meet?"

Sophie smiled. "We met through your mother, in a way."

Marie looked askance at the woman. "My mother? My mother died of cancer when I was eight."

Sophie nodded as if she was perfectly aware of that fact. "And your father missed her horribly."

"She was the world to him. Well, along with me and Drake House. I was worried about him being lonely after I left for college." She'd mostly been worried about him devoting every waking moment to the Drakes, exactly what he hadn't wanted for her. She wished he would have told her he'd met a woman. It would have made her feel so much more at ease. "But I still don't understand how the two of you met through my mother."

Sophie and Chelsea exchanged looks.

"What is it?"

Chelsea shrugged to her aunt and let out a resigned sigh. "You might as well tell her."

"Your father came to me because he believed I could help him communicate with your mother."

"Communicate?" The ground seemed to shift under Marie's feet. "What are you? Some kind of medium?"

"No. Not me. Chelsea has more talent in that area than I have."

Chelsea shot her a warning look. "We don't need to go into that. She's here to learn about her father."

"Yes, your father. He wanted to use a room I have upstairs."

"For what?"

"As a portal to reach your mother."

"A séance?" Marie wasn't buying any of this. Not one word. She couldn't imagine her father holding some sort of séance. If Chelsea wasn't here, looking so serious and grim, she'd chalk up Sophie as a bit of a kook.

"Not exactly a séance. A portal to communicate."

"A room upstairs?"

She nodded. "A special room I've constructed. A room that acts as a door to the spiritual world."

A laugh bubbled through Marie's lips. She covered her mouth with a hand.

"This isn't a joke." Chelsea crossed her arms over her chest. "And my aunt isn't off her rocker, or whatever it is you're thinking."

"I wasn't…" Marie's cheeks heated. Fact was, she'd been thinking exactly that. She focused on the older woman. "I'm sorry. Please explain. I need to understand my father. I know you can help me do that."

Sophie's smile didn't change, as if Marie's disbelief didn't bother or surprise her in the least. "Have you ever heard of a psychomanteum?"

"A what?"

"It's based on a phenomenon we first see in Greek mythology. A psychomanteum or oracle of the dead."

Marie had studied Homer as an undergraduate. "The pool of blood in Odysseus."

Sophie's face brightened with the glow of a teacher who had just broken through to a lagging student. "Exactly. Odysseus dug a pit and filled it with animal blood. Through the reflection in the blood, he could communicate with spirits."

Marie suppressed a shiver. What kind of strange things had her father gotten involved in? "Your attic is filled with blood?"

Now it was Chelsea's turn to cover a smile.

"Oh, heavens, no." Sophie laughed. "You must really think I'm a nut."

Marie's cheeks burned. Her face must be glowing red. "I'm sorry. I didn't mean…I'm just trying to understand."

Sophie laid a comforting hand on Marie's arm. "Of course you are, sweetheart."

"My aunt uses mirrors, not blood," Chelsea explained. "Communicating through a psychomanteum really has quite a long tradition, and it crosses cultures. Africans, Siberians, Native Americans…they all used different forms, whether they were gazing into water or blood. There's even a story about Abraham Lincoln seeing his future reflected in a mirror."

Marie had heard of some of these traditions. It had never occurred to her that they were anything but superstition and myth. "And my father believed he could look into mirrors and contact my mother?"

Sophie's smile widened. "He didn't just believe it. He did it."

"He did it? He contacted my mother?" Marie shook her head. This was impossible. Ridiculous. "What did my mother say?"

"She didn't *say* anything. The psychomanteum experience isn't like some séance you see in a movie, dear. A ghost doesn't just appear and recite his or her life story. Not usually, anyway. It's a bit more subtle than that."

"How does it work?"

"It's more like meditation, opening yourself to stimuli we don't pick up normally."

"So my father meditated by staring into a mirror, and he spoke with my mother?"

"He sensed your mother. He could feel she was there. He could feel her happiness that he'd met me."

So that's what this was about? Sophie was worried Marie wouldn't approve of her relationship with her father and she thought some spiritual mumbo jumbo would help her cause? "I don't know about any psychowhatever, but I'm glad he met you. I really am. I was worried about him after I left for school. Worried he'd be lonely. And he was. For years."

"That means a lot to me, honey." Sophie's expression shifted. "But your mother's acceptance wasn't all he experienced in the psychomanteum. There were other things. Not-so-pleasant things."

"About my mother?" A shiver raced along Marie's nerves. Weird. She didn't believe any of this, yet Sophie's comment and tone of voice left her cold.

"Aunt Sophie…" Chelsea's voice held a warning ring.

Her aunt splayed her hands out in front of her. "She needs to know what Edwin experienced. She's here to look into his murder."

Marie's chill turned to shock. "How did you know that? Did the police chief—"

"Police Chief Hammer?" Chelsea rolled her eyes. "All that man cares about is making his job as easy as possible. A murder might mean that he has to do some actual work."

That certainly jibed with Marie's assessment of the man. "Then how did you know why I'm here?"

Sophie leaned forward and placed her fingers on Marie's arm. "You know your father. He wasn't one to enjoy walking the shoreline."

"Exactly." At least Marie wasn't the only one to recognize something very wrong with the police's accident theory.

Sophie nodded her head, her gray bun bobbing. "Contacting your mother was a good experience. A peaceful experience. The unpleasantness didn't have anything to do with your mother. It had something to do with Drake House."

"Drake House?" Marie's head spun. She held out her hands palms out, trying to physically push back all these bizarre claims and confusing twists of logic.

"Your father learned things in the psychomanteum. Things that upset him."

"What?"

"He wouldn't tell me. He said he didn't want to endanger me, especially after all I went through with Chelsea and her fiancé, Michael."

"Aunt Sophie…" Another warning from Chelsea.

Sophie gave Marie a conspiratorial look. "I'll fill you in on that story sometime." She glanced at Chelsea.

"When I'm not around to stop you?" Chelsea shook her head. "My experiences don't have anything to do with your father, Marie. My aunt just likes telling stories."

Sophie harrumphed at her niece, then returned her focus to Marie. "I wish I could tell you more about what your father experienced, sweetie. All I know is that it upset him greatly. And he said it led him to a dangerous secret."

"A dangerous secret?" The secret that got him killed?

Chelsea nodded as if reading her thoughts. "Your father was murdered to keep him quiet about what he learned."

"How do you know that?"

Chelsea shifted in her seat and glanced at her aunt.

Sophie smiled. "You mean are we basing that theory on fact or on some sort of vision in a mirror?"

"Well…yes."

"*I'm* basing it on what he told me before he died. Edwin was scared for me. He was also scared for his own life."

Sophie's words wound into a hard ball in Marie's chest. She couldn't picture her father frightened. He'd always been so strong, so in control. The only times she'd known him to be truly worried was when her mother was sick…and after he'd witnessed the way she looked at Brandon the summer before she'd left for college.

"I can't reach him in the psychomanteum. I've tried every day since he died, but it's no good. Maybe he's still trying to protect me. Or maybe I'm not the one he needs to communicate with."

The older woman stared at Marie so hard, Marie couldn't fight the urge to shift in her chair. She didn't want to ask what Sophie was getting at. She had a feeling she didn't want to know. "It's getting late. I'd better get back."

"He always talked about how he hadn't seen you in so long, how he had so much he wanted to tell you, so much he needed to say…."

"Aunt Sophie, if she doesn't want to—"

"If your father will communicate with anyone, it will be you, Marie. He loved you so."

Marie shook her head. "I can't possibly. I don't even believe."

"It won't hurt to try."

Marie grabbed the handles of her bag in one fist and thrust herself out of her chair. "I really have to go." She picked up her coat from the sofa arm where Sophie had draped it.

"It's not ghostly, Marie. Forget about all those movies you've seen. That was horror. This is real life."

"I'm sorry. I don't mean any disrespect, Sophie, really I don't. Talking to ghosts might be your real life, but it's not mine." She pulled on her coat and hurried out the front door and down the steps, nearly tripping over her own feet in her rush to get away.

THE MAIN FLOOR of Drake House was dark by the time Marie drove back through the gate, down the winding drive and parked in the empty servants' lot next to the carriage house. Dinner having been served, the servants had no doubt returned to their own homes. She looked up at the light in the private eastern wing of the house. The master suite, among other rooms. Brandon was home. She couldn't help but wonder what he was doing.

Thinking of her?

Pushing away that idea, she started through the east garden to the kitchen entrance. After recovering from her experience at Sophie's and grabbing a dinner of crab cakes at one of the harbor restaurants, she'd debated skipping Drake House and heading straight for the bed-and-breakfast off Main Street where she'd reserved a room. In the end, she'd decided she wouldn't be able to sleep, anyway, not after her conversation with Sophie and her niece. If she did slip into sleep, she'd spend the night hashing out their strange ideas in her dreams.

Better to get to work on her father's suite and keep her mind off both ghosts *and* Brandon Drake.

Marie followed the curvy path made of loose white shells. The night was dark, but she didn't need light to see where she was going. Even after ten years, she knew Drake House the way she knew her own heart. Even though some details had changed, there was something about this house and its grounds she recognized deep inside. Something that would be with her forever. Like the tune her mother always hummed. Like the almost imperceptible twinkle in her father's dry smile.

She swallowed into a tight throat. She missed him so much. Her father was so much a part of Drake House, she could still feel him, even outside on the grounds. The next few days, being in his rooms, sorting through his things, weren't going to be easy. But at least she'd feel closer to him. Just being back on the estate made her feel closer.

The night was warm for December, yet pockets of cold, still air dotted the path, raising goose bumps on her skin. She rubbed her arms and quickened her pace. She probably could have parked in the lot near the grand entrance and cut through the inside of the house to the butler's quarters. But somehow that felt presumptuous, as if she thought she belonged at Drake House or was some sort of honored guest. Here in Jenkins Cove, she was the butler's daughter, pure and simple. In the past ten years, she had learned her place.

She circled the corner of the east wing and approached the back entrance. A light glowed from a set of windows off the kitchen. Her father's quarters.

Her steps faltered.

The light dimmed and shifted. Not lamplight. More like a flashlight beam.

Was someone searching through her father's rooms?

A flutter of nerves made her feel sick to her stomach. Who would gain from searching her father's quarters? A murderer trying to cover his tracks?

The light flicked off. Darkness draped the house.

Marie pressed her lips into a hard line and covered her mouth with her hand. Whoever it was, the last thing she wanted was for the intruder to know he'd been spotted. She stepped off the path and slipped behind a holly bush. Reaching into her purse, she grasped the keys Shelley had given her, threading them between her fingers so they protruded like spikes from her fist.

The kitchen door closed with a click. Marie peered through spined leaves. A figure wearing a boxy rain slicker crossed the porch and descended the steps to the path. The hood covered the intruder's face, and the size of the slicker made it impossible to discern the size or shape of the person beneath. The figure turned in her direction.

Marie pressed back behind the bush, hoping the night was dark enough, the evergreen bush thick enough to hide her. The rhythmic crunch of footsteps on oyster shells approached…slowed…stopped.

She drew in a breath and held it.

Suddenly darkness rushed at her. Hands grabbed her shoulders. A fist slammed into her jaw. Leaves clawed at her like frantic fingers.

A scream tore from her throat.

Chapter Four

Brandon relived it almost every night. Fighting his way into the blazing car. Choking on smoke and gasoline. Charlotte's scream ringing in his ears. Helpless to save her.

He jolted up from the window seat, surprised he was in his room, no fire around him. No choking smoke. No Charlotte.

The scream came again.

Not Charlotte. Not a dream.

"Oh my God. Marie."

He thrust to his feet. His leg faltered, folding under him, and he grabbed the window molding for balance. He snatched his cane. Willing the damn limb to function, he bolted for the door. Clutching the carved railing with his free hand, he thundered down the back stairs and sprang into the parlor. He moved through the dining room, half hopping, half galloping. He had to move faster.

He raced through the kitchen and burst out the door. The night was dark, no moon, no light. He couldn't see a thing. Couldn't hear a thing but the rasp of his own breath. He held the cane out in front of him like a weapon. "Marie? Who's out here? Marie?"

A quiet groan emanated from a tall hedge of holly near the path leading into the east garden. "I'm here. I'm okay."

Pressure bore down on his chest. Her voice sounded small, shaken. Not at all okay. He followed the sound. He couldn't see her at first, but he could feel her. He could smell the scent of her shampoo. Something both spicy and sweet. Something that reminded him of a warm summer and good times. "Where are you?"

"Here." Holly leaves rustled. She sat at the bush's base, struggling to free herself from sharp leaves.

As he reached for her hand, his heart felt as if it would burst from his chest. "Can you get up?"

"I think so…yes."

She grasped his fingers, and he pulled her to her feet. "What happened?"

She focused on him, round caramel-colored eyes in a pale face. "Someone was sneaking around in the house. An intruder. He saw me."

"He attacked you?"

She lifted her fingers to her jaw. "He hit me…I think."

Brandon tried to discern the discoloration of a bruise, but it was too dark.

"I saw a light in my father's quarters. When I heard the kitchen door close, I hid."

"In a holly bush?" He could see something dark on her cheek, feel something slightly sticky on the hand he clutched in his, probably blood. No doubt the sharp edges of the leaves had scratched her up pretty good.

"I hid behind the bush, not inside the bush. When he hit me, I fell."

"Let's get you inside." Still gripping her hand, he led her toward the open kitchen door.

"What are you going to do?"

"Call the police."

"What are you going to tell them? I didn't see his face. I don't even know if it was a him."

"I'll take care of it." He hurried Marie up the steps and into the house. Closing the door, he locked it behind them. He didn't know what the police could do, but he wanted them there. If nothing else, they could check out the grounds and make sure the bastard who attacked Marie was gone.

He turned to look at her. In the light of the kitchen, he could see the pink shadow of a bruise bloom along her jaw. The holly had scratched one cheek as it had her hands. Beads of blood dotted the slashes. Snags and runs spoiled her black tights. "You're hurt."

"You should have seen the other guy." She tried for a smile, but it turned into a flinch of pain.

"Let me see." He brushed her hair back from her cheek with his fingertips. Her skin was soft. Her hair smelled like…cinnamon. That's what it was. Like the cinnamon gum she'd chewed as a teen. He took a deep breath. In the back of his mind he recognized the clatter of his cane falling to the floor.

"Does it look bad?"

He forced himself to focus on her injuries. "Not too bad. I'll get some ice for that bruise. And there's a first aid kit here somewhere. I'll get those scrapes cleaned."

"I can do it."

He met her eyes and swallowed into a dry throat. What was he thinking? He was having a hard enough time touching her skin and smelling her hair without doing or saying something he'd regret. Playing nurse-maid would send him over the edge. "Of course. I'll find the kit for you."

Her lips trembled. "I can get it. My father always kept it in the same place."

"Yes, all right." Come to think of it, he had no idea where Edwin kept the first aid supplies. He had even less of an idea what he thought he was doing hovering over Marie. He needed to step away from her, to focus on something other than the way her hair smelled and the warmth of her body and the tremble in her lips. But right this minute, she was all he could see.

He bent down and picked up his cane. Pulling in a measured breath, he stepped to the burglar alarm and punched in the activation code.

"Do you usually have the alarm on at night?"

He nodded, but didn't allow himself to look at her. He'd only be back to hovering if he did, noticing things he couldn't let himself notice. "I told Shelley to leave it off for you."

"So Shelley knew it was off. Who else?"

"Isabella. Maybe Josef. Anyone who knew you were planning to come back tonight, I guess. I doubt any of them would be looking to break in. They're in and out of here all day."

"The man you were talking to when I was here earlier? Did he know the alarm would be off?"

"Doug Heller? Maybe. Yeah, he was probably still here when I talked to Shelley." Something was going on. Something Marie didn't want to tell him. Despite his better judgment, he turned around and eyed her. "What are you getting at, Marie?"

"Do you think it's just a coincidence someone broke in the one night the alarm was off?"

"Good point. I'll mention it to the police. But I can't

see the staff involved in some kind of break-in. Or Heller, for that matter."

She shrugged a shoulder, the gesture a little too stiff. She was working on some sort of theory about the break-in. A theory she obviously didn't want to share with him.

Not that he could blame her. She'd trusted him with more than a theory before, and he'd thrown her to the dogs. She'd be smart to never trust him again.

"I've got to make that call. Whoever attacked you could still be out there." He made his way to the household office and plucked the cordless phone from its charger. He stared at the receiver in his hand. He didn't want the hoopla of calling 9-1-1. But he didn't even know where Edwin kept the phone book. Without Edwin, it seemed he couldn't handle a damn thing.

Glancing back to the kitchen, he let the idea of asking Marie sit in his mind for less than a second. The feeling he'd gotten when near her still vibrated deep in his bones. When she was close, she was all he could focus on. When he was touching her, the sensations were so strong they were painful.

After Charlotte's death, he'd wished he could no longer feel. Not the torment of his injuries, not the guilt in his heart, not the emptiness that hadn't been filled in far too long. Now that Marie was back, now that she was here in Drake House, he couldn't do anything *but* feel.

He had to keep control of himself. And if that meant staying away from her, he'd find a way.

He called up the directory feature on the phone. Sure enough, Edwin had programed the police department's nonemergency number. His butler had saved him yet again. If he wasn't so shaken by everything that had happened tonight, he'd find that ironic.

"Jenkins Cove Police Department," an official-sounding woman answered. "What is the nature of your call?"

"I'd like to report a possible burglary at Drake House."

"Mr. Drake?"

"Yes."

"Will you hold, Mr. Drake? The chief is here right now. He'd like to talk to you himself."

"Sure." Brandon frowned into the phone. It wasn't unusual for the chief to personally handle anything having to do with Brandon or his uncle Cliff. He supposed that was what happened when your family had nearly single handedly established and nurtured a small town like Jenkins Cove. Parks were named after you. Statues of your father and grandfather and generations back graced the town square. And the chief of police personally handled your crime reports. Still, it was awfully late for the chief to be in. It must have something to do with the state police's investigation of the mass grave that had been found just down the road.

"Brandon," Chief Hammer's voice boomed over the phone. "I hear you had a break-in. I hope no damage was done."

Damage. Brandon had been so absorbed with Marie he hadn't even looked for damage. He stepped out into the kitchen and swept it with his gaze. "None that I've noticed."

"Glad to hear that. We've had problems with some teens in the area. Vandalism. You might have read about it in the *Gazette*."

Brandon had read about a lot of wild things in the *Gazette* lately, with the coverage of the mass grave, the doctor who was rumored to be responsible and his lackey the state police had hauled off into custody. A lot more excitement than usual in Jenkins Cove. The teen delinquent stories must have been buried on a later page. "I know my uncle Cliff has had some problems with vandals. Let me look around to be sure there's nothing damaged."

Getting a grip on himself, he made his way to Edwin's suite. The door was open and Marie stood in the sitting room, her back to him. He forced himself to notice the room's condition and that of the two bedrooms beyond, not the curve of her hips in the skirt and sweater, now that she'd taken off her coat. "Notice anything missing or damaged?"

Marie shook her head. "No. I don't think so, anyway."

He nodded and forced his attention back to the phone. "The rooms we think the burglar entered don't seem disturbed."

"We?" Hammer repeated over the phone.

"Edwin Leonard's daughter, Marie, is packing up his things."

"I see."

"She saw the light on in the butler's quarters. The burglar attacked her trying to get away."

"Is she all right?"

"Just a bruise and a few scratches."

"This is going to seem like an odd question, Brandon, but are you sure someone was in the house?"

Brandon paused. "Of course I'm sure."

"Did you see anything yourself? Hear anything?"

"What are you getting at, Chief?"

"Nothing. I'm just a little concerned about Marie

Leonard. I had a talk with her today at the funeral, and she seemed to be having a bad time of it."

Brandon cupped a hand over the phone and stepped out of the room. He wasn't sure what Hammer was getting at, but he knew he didn't want Marie to overhear. "Her father died. Of course she's upset. You think it's more than that?"

"I'd call her paranoid."

"Paranoid?" Not a word he would associate with Marie. If anything she'd seemed too calm, too in control. But then, he'd been so turned inside out since he'd first seen her this afternoon, maybe she was just controlled in comparison. "What is she paranoid about?"

"She seems to think someone killed her father."

His words probably should have surprised Brandon, but they didn't. They explained a lot. "Why does she think that?"

"You'll have to ask her. I'm afraid it isn't based in reality. I've found no evidence that Edwin Leonard was murdered."

Of course, knowing Hammer, he hadn't expended much effort looking. "Thanks for the heads-up, Chief. But no matter what is going on with Marie, I don't think she imagined this attack."

"I'm not saying she did. I'm concerned about her. That's all."

"Well, if you could send someone out here, I can guarantee Ms. Leonard would feel a whole lot better. And so would I."

"Soon as I can, Brandon. I only have two officers on tonight, and one is securing the state police's dig site. It might be the state's investigation, but you wouldn't believe the monkey wrench it's thrown into our day-to-day operations."

Brandon grimaced. Apparently the chief hadn't had a good few days, either. "Send someone out as soon as you can. I want to make sure whoever it was is gone."

"In the meantime, stay inside, make sure your doors are locked and turn on that fancy alarm system of yours just to be on the safe side."

"Already done." He turned off the phone. The only problem with the chief's advice was the idea of locking himself in with Marie. Still, he couldn't see how he was going to find it within himself to let her leave, not when whoever had attacked her might still be outside.

"Is an officer on the way?"

Something jumped in his chest at the sound of her voice. He looked up to see her standing in the doorway to Edwin's quarters. "It might take a while. You have a place to stay?"

"A B&B in Jenkins Cove."

"How long are you planning to hang around yet tonight?" Edwin Leonard was an impeccably neat and organized man. Still, he'd been the butler of Drake House since before Brandon was born. Cleaning out his rooms was going to be a big job.

"I'll be here a few hours at least. I don't think I can sleep after all this."

He was sure he wouldn't be sleeping, either. But at least he had the sense not to offer to help. "Why don't you stay?"

She raised her brows.

"In your old room. Edwin would have insisted. And I would feel better if you didn't go back outside. Not until the police have a chance to check out the grounds."

He had to be crazy, inviting her to stay under his roof. Drake House was big, but not big enough to keep him from listening for her all night long and noting her every movement.

At least that way he could keep her safe. Edwin would have insisted on that as well.

"Thanks."

"Chief Hammer is concerned about you."

She twisted her lips to one side. "I'll bet he is."

"Why?"

She waved her hand in front of her face as if trying to erase the words between them. "Nothing. Never mind. It's just been a long day, that's all."

"He said you believe your father was murdered."

She held his gaze but said nothing, as if waiting for some kind of prompt.

"I take it you do. Why?"

"My father never walked near the water. You know that. He was deathly afraid of water."

"So he couldn't have accidently fallen in."

He wasn't sure if she'd nodded or not. She just watched him as if waiting for him to discount her theory.

"Hammer says there's no evidence."

"Because he's too lazy to find it."

That was the Charles Hammer he knew. If the answer wasn't easy, Hammer wasn't interested. "So that's why you're here."

"I'm here to pack up my father's things."

"And look for evidence he was murdered. And that's what you think our burglar tonight was doing, too, don't you? Looking for something incriminating. Something that ties him to Edwin's murder."

Again she didn't react. She just seemed to be sizing him up, watching, waiting. For what? Did she think he was going to tell her she was wrong? Hell, it should have occurred to him earlier how unlikely it was for Edwin to venture close to the water. He should have been looking for explanations himself. "Talk to me, Marie. Maybe I can help."

She didn't look convinced.

"Well, there's no reason for you to tie up a room at the B&B during Christmas shopping season. You can stay here as long as you need. Shelley gave you keys?"

"Just to the kitchen entrance and my father's quarters."

Leave it to Shelley. The day he'd promoted her to fill Edwin's job, she'd collected keys from all employees, doling them out only when she deemed necessary. The woman wielded her new power with a closed fist. "I'll get you a complete set."

"Thanks." Her lips softened. Not quite a smile, but an acknowledgment. Something.

"It's the least I can do. Your father meant a lot to me." *And so do you.* The words stuck in his throat. Not that he would ever say them out loud. He'd hurt too many people the last time he'd given in to that indulgence. Himself, Marie, and Charlotte most of all. He deserved the pain. But Charlotte… He couldn't erase what he'd done to her. Nor would he risk hurting Marie again. No matter what happened, he had to protect her. He owed Edwin. And he definitely owed her. "I'll go wait for the police. Good night, Marie."

MARIE LAUNCHED into the fifth drawer of her father's personal desk. So far she'd found nothing. No questionable photos or letters or anything that even hinted why someone might want him dead. But she had gone through almost a half box of tissues wiping the tears that continuously leaked from her eyes.

What she wouldn't give to have him back.

She closed her eyes, her lids swollen and hot. She didn't know what she'd do without him. Ten years ago, he'd helped her put her life in perspective. He'd hugged away her tears in that stiff-backed way he had. He'd encouraged her to get away from Drake House and make the life she deserved.

She hadn't lived with him for over ten years, but she knew whenever she had a question, whenever she needed to know if she was making the right decision, he was only a phone call away. Without him, she felt lost.

If only she could talk to him about her stirred-up feelings for Brandon.

She rubbed her eyes. She knew what her father would say. He would tell her to go home. To get away from Brandon, from Drake House. The same thing he'd told her ten years ago.

Too bad she couldn't follow his advice this time. Not until she found out who killed him. Not until she brought his murderer to justice.

She reached to the top of the desk and snapped on the ancient transistor radio she remembered her father using to listen to his beloved Orioles on summer nights. She turned her attention to the last desk drawer. "I'll Be Home for Christmas" drifted over the airwaves.

Great.

Here she was. Home for Christmas. Except the only person she had to come home to was gone. Taken away forever.

She turned the dial. Static took over.

Fabulous.

She twisted the knob. Now she couldn't get a signal at all. She rubbed a hand over her eyes. She was too tired for this. Maybe she should get some sleep and finish going through the desk tomorrow. She reached up to switch the radio off. Shadows of a voice rustled among the white noise. "Murder."

Marie jerked her hand back.

"Murder."

There it was again. A whisper rising from the static.

Marie frowned at the radio. It had to be a news report. Maybe something about the mass grave the state police were investigating, the one the waitress in the crab shack had been buzzing about last night. Marie gave the dial a twist, moving the needle back and forth, trying to get better reception. The static fuzzed on.

"Marie."

The whisper again. Saying her name?

She snapped the radio off. Sophie Caldwell's theories about communicating with ghosts flitting through her mind, she thrust herself to her feet and walked into the bathroom. She was tired and she was imagining things. That was all it was. All it could be.

Turning on the water to warm, she fished a hair band from her bag and pulled her bob back from her face. She looked into the mirror.

Sophie and Chelsea believed mirrors were like oracles. A way to see into the spiritual world. A way to communicate with loved ones lost.

The only image in her mirror was herself with her hair in a hair band. Not her best look.

She thrust cupped hands into the warm water and

lifted it to splash her face. She froze before the water reached her skin.

That scent.

Marie took a long breath. She knew the smell. The fragrance was faint, but she recognized the exotic notes, a blend dominated by jasmine.

She let the water drain between her fingers.

Pressure lodged under her rib cage, hard as a balled fist. Glancing around the bathroom, she dried her hands on a towel and turned off the tap.

The scent had to be caused by soap or air freshener. But look as she might, she didn't see a source. As she searched, the scent grew stronger. She could swear it was coming from the other side of the bathroom door.

A tremor moved through her chest. Her pulse thrummed in her ears.

She'd remember that scent all her life. And the woman who wore it. So exotic, so sophisticated. And so much more than little Marie Leonard. More beautiful, more accomplished. In every way, more.

No wonder Brandon had made her his wife.

But Charlotte had died six months ago. Why was Marie smelling her scent now? Here in the butler's quarters?

Sophie and Chelsea had talked about spirits communicating through images in mirrors, not voices carried on radio static, not scents. She was freaking herself out over nothing…wasn't she?

Pulse thrumming in her ears, she stepped out into her father's sitting room. The room was as vacant as before. She tested the air again. The scent was stronger, but it didn't seem to be coming from this room, either.

She followed her nose to the door leading to the estate office and kitchen area. The cloud cover had cleared outside, and stainless steel and stone counter-tops stretched long and cold in ribbons of feeble moon-light shining through window blinds. The scent was even stronger out here. It teased the air as if Charlotte had just walked through the room.

Ridiculous.

More likely Brandon had the furnace filters treated with the scent to remind him of Charlotte. Or Shelley used jasmine air fresheners to memorialize the mistress she adored, à la Mrs. Danvers from Daphne du Maurier's *Rebecca*. A giggle bubbled up in Marie's throat. She was being absurd, letting her imagination run away with her—first to ghosts and now to characters from novels. Silly or not, she followed the scent.

Marie wove her way through the kitchen and veered through the hall and into the dining room. She circled the grand table and stepped quietly across the parquet floor and oriental rugs in the first-floor sitting room. A hint of moonlight filtered through draperies, creating misty images on leaded mirrors. Images that almost looked like ghosts.

"Marie?" Brandon's voice boomed from the shadows. "What is it?"

Marie started. She whirled around to see him jolt up from a sofa in the sitting room.

His eyelids looked heavy, as if he'd just awakened. He reached for his cane and walked toward her. He stopped just inches away. Close enough for her to trail her fingertips over his stubbled chin and the slick, scarred skin of his cheek.

Marie's nerves jangled. For a moment she couldn't think.

His dark eyebrows dipped with concern. "Is something wrong?"

Something? *Everything* was wrong. Him standing so close. Her need to touch him, to hold him, to pretend the past ten years had never happened. She shook her head. "Don't you smell that scent?"

"What is it? Something burning?"

"No. It's like perfume. Jasmine." Maybe Brandon was used to it. Maybe he didn't even detect it anymore. Marie took another deep draw. The fragrance had faded, but the whisper of it was still there. "I noticed it in my father's room and followed it out here. Don't you smell it?"

"Jasmine?"

"It was the scent Charlotte used to wear."

His mouth flattened in a hard line. She could see him moving away from her, withdrawing, even though he hadn't physically moved an inch. "Why are you saying this?"

Realization hit her with the force of a slap across the face. She'd blurted out what was in her mind without any thought about who she was talking to, how bringing up his dead wife would make him feel. Her lack of tact knew no bounds.

She took a step backward as heat crept over her cheeks. "I'm sorry. I got carried away."

"Carried away by what?"

"My imagination, I guess. The house. The conversation I had with Sophie Caldwell."

"You talked about Charlotte?"

She shook her head. "We talked about ghosts."

If she'd thought he had given her a cold look before, she was mistaken. The temperature in the room dropped twenty degrees.

She'd better at least try to explain. "They wanted me to try to contact my father."

"That crazy psychomanteum of theirs?"

"I guess." She wished she could crawl under a rock. "I'm sorry for bringing up Charlotte. I just heard a voice and smelled that scent and my imagination went a little wild, I think."

"A voice?"

She shook her head again. She didn't want him to get the wrong impression. "On the radio. It was nothing. Like I said, just my imagination."

His lips softened. "You've been through a lot. Don't worry about it."

His kindness did more to rattle her than even his anger. "I didn't mean to… I'm going to go to bed now."

He leaned toward her, as if he wanted to touch her but didn't quite dare. "Let me help you."

Help her go to bed? She knew that wasn't what he meant, but another giggle bubbled up inside her, anyway. Fatigue. Hysteria. She choked it back.

Brandon didn't seem to realize her struggle. He looked at her with that same concerned look. A look that made her want to curl up in his arms and cry.

Finally he let out a heavy breath. "There's no reason you have to look into Edwin's death alone. I know people. I can help."

All she could manage was a nod.

"Has Hammer given you a copy of the accident report?"

"Yes." She forced a word out. A miracle.

"How about the autopsy?"

"No."

"What do you say tomorrow we go to Baltimore and have a talk with the medical examiner?"

"You can do that? I called, and his secretary or assistant or whatever gave me the runaround."

"I'll give him a call. He'll make time."

"Of course." The world worked differently for Brandon than it did for her. There were perks to being a Drake.

"Like I said before, Edwin was important to me, too. Very important." He gave her a controlled nod. "Tomorrow morning, then?"

Marie took a deep breath. The scent was gone. Even though the desire to touch Brandon still pulsed through her veins, she felt focused once again. Focused on her father, on finding his killer, on bringing his murderer to justice. As long as she could remember why she was here, she could handle the rest.

Even being around Brandon Drake. "See you tomorrow."

Chapter Five

By the time Marie ate Shelley's wonderful breakfast of crab benedict and rode to Baltimore in the quiet comfort of Brandon's chauffeured car, she was beginning to understand just how different Brandon's life was from her own. And when the Maryland medical examiner was actually waiting to talk to them, she knew accepting Brandon's help had been the right thing to do.

Or at least she hoped.

She concentrated on the harsh disinfectant and repulsive fleshy smells of the morgue. Staff bustled through the halls clad in baggy scrubs, some wearing stiff long-sleeved aprons over top. The distraction didn't work. She didn't have to look at Brandon to feel him next to her. She didn't have to smell the leather of his jacket to be aware of every move he made.

His almost black hair glistened in the fluorescent light. His black leather car coat accentuated his broad shoulders as if it were made for him alone. Of course, it probably was. Even his cane only played up the aristocratic air about him.

No wonder she'd fallen so hard when she was a

teenager. Good thing she knew better than to trust the emotions he brought out in her now.

The medical examiner was waiting for them when they entered his office. An older man with skin that resembled a wrinkled brown paper bag, he motioned for them to take off their coats and sit in a pair of chairs facing the desk. Brandon made introductions, and Marie shook the man's hand.

After the formalities were finished, Dr. Tracy started flipping through a pile of file folders lying on his bland, government-issue desk. "I'm sorry I haven't had time to pull your father's records from the recent cases. This will just take a second. Your town has been keeping us awfully busy lately, what with the state police excavation site."

After reading the first few articles back in Michigan, Marie had avoided the story of the mass grave, even though it was in papers and on news channels all over the country. The whole thing was too upsetting. Too depressing. The thought that all those people were victimized just because they wanted a better life. The thought that a doctor who'd sworn to do no harm had forced them to give up organs in return for their passage into the country. The thought that many had given their lives through no choice of their own, their hollow shells dumped into mass graves.

She shuddered. "They caught the men responsible for that, didn't they?"

"One is dead and now the other…" Dr. Tracy peered over his reading glasses at Marie, his hands still shuffling through a stack of reports. "You haven't heard."

"Heard what?"

"Franz Kreeger, the one who was jailed. They found him dead this morning."

Brandon's eyebrows dipped low. "Suicide?"

"I don't know. But I guess I'll find out."

Marie nodded, realizing that what the doctor said was literally true. He would find out, personally. Or at least he would with the help of his staff. Just as his staff would examine each of the bodies buried outside Jenkins Cove. "Have they recovered all the bodies from the mass grave?"

He shook his head. "They're bringing in new ones every day. Very old ones. Fresh ones. It seems like they'd need more than two men to do all that damage. Not that I'm speculating." He pulled a file from the pack and set the others aside. Adjusting his glasses, he flipped open the folder. "Now, how can I help?"

She paused, waiting for Brandon to speak. Instead, he gave her an encouraging nod.

She cleared her throat. "The police told me my father's death was an accident."

"And you want to know if it really was?"

"Yes."

"I can't tell you that."

"Can't tell me?" Marie slumped against the back of her chair. How could that be? "Don't you determine cause of death?"

"Yes. That's exactly what I try to do. And your father's cause of death was drowning."

Marie's throat tightened. Her father had always hated water. He'd always been scared to death of it. The fact that he'd drowned was unspeakably cruel.

"The police believe Edwin hit his head and fell in the water," Brandon said. "Is that possible?"

Marie pressed her lips into a grateful half smile. At this moment, she wasn't sure she could talk. Not unless she wanted to start bawling.

"Yes. He had an injury to the back of his head that could be considered consistent with that theory."

Marie tilted her head to the side. It sounded as though the medical examiner wasn't quite sure the police were on the right track.

Of course, that could just be what she wanted to hear. She forced her voice to remain steady. "Could it have happened differently?"

"Yes. When I say something is consistent with the police's theory, that doesn't mean their story of the death is the only one possible." The doctor glanced down at the report and then pointed to his own bald head. His finger stopped near the top. "The bruising occurred right about here."

"Did he have other bruising that suggested he fell on the rocks? Like on his back or shoulders?"

"No. He had some scrapes on his legs, but that could have been caused by the rocks after he was in the water."

Marie swallowed into an aching throat. She knew the doctor was trained to look at her father's death—any death—in an objective and emotionless way. But it was impossible for her to listen to these details with the same detachment. She was just glad, once again, that Brandon was with her.

Brandon narrowed his eyes on the doctor's head as if trying to visualize what had happened to her father that night. "So he would have had to fall nearly upside down. As if he went off the pier in a somersault and didn't make it all the way over."

The doctor nodded. "That could explain it."

Marie shook her head. That wasn't how she imagined it happening. That wasn't it at all. "He was hit from behind."

The doctor looked down at the report, then back to Marie. His expression was matter-of-fact, as if her statement didn't surprise him at all. "The bruising is such that he could have been hit from behind."

A trill vibrated up Marie's backbone. This was what she had come to find. Something that would prove he was murdered. Some kind of evidence Chief Hammer would have to acknowledge. "Will you tell the Jenkins Cove police chief that?"

Dr. Tracy's forehead furrowed. His lips took on a sympathetic slant. "Just because it's possible doesn't mean it happened that way."

"But it's more likely than my father walking along the water and doing a somersault onto the rocks."

The medical examiner waved his hands in the air between them, as if clearing out the words they'd spoken. "What I'm saying, Ms. Leonard, is I can't tell exactly how your father hit his head before he drowned. It could have happened exactly the way the police said. If you're looking for evidence he was murdered, this is not going to do it."

Marie lifted her eyes from the document in the doctor's hands and stared at the overhead lights. She couldn't let herself cry. She knew her father was murdered. The ambiguity of the autopsy results didn't change that. She'd just have to find better evidence. She'd have to dig harder.

But where to look next?

"Thank you for your time, Doctor." Brandon thrust out a hand. The men shook.

Marie stretched her hand out as well. Swallowing the emotion welling inside, she forced her voice to remain steady. "I appreciate your candor."

The doctor enfolded her hand in his. His graying brow furrowed in concern, as if he could sense how close she was to losing control. "If you have any further questions, you know how to reach me."

"Yes." She turned away and made for the door, needing to escape the smells, the emotion, the doctor's concern more than she remembered needing anything. Brandon slipped a gentle arm around her waist, and at his tender touch, her tears started to flow.

BRANDON HANDED Marie the pressed handkerchief Edwin always insisted he carry and guided her out of the morgue. He'd been amazed she'd been able to hold back her grief this long. While he hated to see her cry, he knew it would be better for her to let it out.

He spotted Josef waiting on a side street and flagged him to bring the town car over. The car sidled up to the curb, and Brandon helped Marie inside.

They were humming down the interstate skirting Annapolis by the time Marie composed herself enough to talk. "I'm sorry."

"Don't apologize. If Edwin was my father, I wouldn't be holding it together half as well as you are."

"That's not true. I'm a mess."

He wiped a tear from her cheek with his fingers. Despite his better judgment, he let his fingers linger, soaking up the satin feel of her skin, the warmth. Both he and Marie had lost their mothers when they were young. Ten years ago they'd connected through their shared experience. Even then he'd been impressed how strong and accepting she'd been of her mother's passing. And he knew how much she loved her father. "You're a lot of things, Marie. A mess isn't one of them."

"I don't know about that. I feel like I can't think straight."

That's how he felt, too, at least when he was this close to Marie. And he knew it had nothing to do with grief.

"I can't stand to think of him as just some case in a… It's just so hard."

He moved his fingertips over her cheek to her chin.

She tilted her face up to him. Her eyes glistened. Tears clumped her lashes. Her lips parted.

He leaned toward her. Kissing her right now felt like the most natural thing in the world. As though it was meant to be. Yet that didn't make it any less impossible.

Especially now.

He dropped his hand from her chin and stared straight ahead through the windshield. The Bay Bridge stretched in front of them, twin ribbons of steel curving high above the wide blue of the Chesapeake.

"Can you do me a favor?" Marie's voice sounded pinched.

"Anything."

"When we get back to Jenkins Cove, will you drop me at Thornton Garden Center? It's over—"

"I know where it is." She must want to see Lexie Thornton. Lexie had decorated Drake House for the annual Christmas Ball every year since she'd started working in her parents' business. And just this fall, Edwin had hired her to redesign the east garden. Brandon had forgotten she was Marie's childhood friend. He was relieved Marie still had a friend in the area. No doubt she needed a shoulder to cry on. He only wished it could be his. "Josef?"

The chauffeur nodded. "Thornton Garden Center. Yes, sir."

Chapter Six

Located on the edge of town in a redbrick building off Main Street, Thornton Garden Center was decked out like a Christmas wonderland. Pine bough swags and wreaths were draped dark and fragrant behind clusters of red, white, pink and blue poinsettias. Gold and silver ornaments filled baskets and decorated sample trees. And a variety of holiday-themed and other sun catchers filled wide windows, sparkling like curtains of colored and sculpted ice.

Marie pushed back memories of past Christmases amidst the grand decor of Drake House and entered the center. More decorations cluttered the inside, competing with flower pots, garden orbs and birdbaths waiting for spring. "Carol of the Bells" tinkled in the pine-scented air.

A man in jeans and a heavy sweater looked up from a stack of boxes he was unpacking. Ornate sleighs made of gold wire scattered the countertop in front of him. He held a price gun in one work-roughened hand. "Can I help you?"

"Is Lexie around?"

"She's in the back room working. If you wait just a second, I'll get her for you."

"You look busy. I'll just peek in myself, if you don't mind. I'm Marie Leonard. We're old friends."

His rough brow furrowed. "Any relation to Edwin Leonard?"

"My father."

"I'm sorry. I did some work for him at Drake House. He was a good man."

Marie gave him what she hoped was a grateful smile and nod. After the emotional upheaval she'd gone through in the morgue and in the car with Brandon, she didn't trust herself to talk. The last thing she needed was more tears. "I'll just go back." She turned away before he had the chance to say anything more. Reaching the small workroom, she peeked her head inside.

Lexie stood at a table strewn with pine boughs and ribbon. She attached a luxurious gold bow to a Christmas wreath.

Only a day had passed since Marie had seen Lexie at her father's service, but after all that had happened, she was so relieved to see her friend, it felt as if it had been weeks. "You told me to stop in. I hope my timing is okay."

"Marie. Your timing is perfect. I'm just finishing these up to bring to a client." Lexie set the wreath down, circled the table and took Marie's hands in hers. "Are you okay?"

Marie tried her best to smile. After her latest bout of crying, her nose was sore and her eyelids felt like over-filled sausage casings. She must look horrible. "I'm fine."

Lexie looked doubtful. "I'm not buying it."

The hazards of having a best friend. Even after all this time, Lexie could see right through her. Once again, tears threatened to break free. She shook her head. "How much can one person cry?"

Lexie surrounded her in a hug. "You lost your dad, Marie. Grieving is normal."

Marie nodded, her cheek snug to Lexie's shoulder. If anyone knew about grief, it was Lexie. Marie and Brandon could never be together, but at least she knew he was living his life, albeit without her.

And that was precisely why she'd needed to see Lexie this afternoon.

She pulled out of her friend's embrace and looked her straight in the eye. "You might think I've lost it, but I have a favor to ask you."

"I would never think you'd lost anything."

"Wait until you hear the favor."

"Okay, shoot."

"Do you know anything about the woman who owns House of the Seven Gables?"

"The bed-and-breakfast? Sure. Sophie Caldwell. She comes into the shop. I helped with some of the decorating for their big holiday open house. What about her?"

"She has a way to communicate with people who have died." She told Lexie about the psychomanteum.

Marie waited to see the skeptical look sweep over Lexie's features. It didn't. Instead, she nodded. "You want to try to speak to your father."

Marie teared up, this time with relief. "You don't think that's weird?"

Lexie shrugged. "Weird? No. I'm not convinced it will work, but I think it's natural for you to want to talk to your dad, to say goodbye."

"That's not all I want to say."

"You want to ask him how to handle Brandon Drake?"

Marie choked back a bitter laugh. She could still feel the heat of Brandon's fingertips on her cheek, her chin. And her chest still ached from the way he'd pulled back. She didn't know if she wanted to talk about Brandon. Not even with Lexie. "My father would tell me to handle him by staying far, far away. And he would be right."

Lexie nodded to a nearby window. "I saw his car drop you off. And I heard you were staying at Drake House. It doesn't seem like you're staying very far away."

So much for avoiding the subject of Brandon. She'd forgotten how quickly news could travel in a small town like Jenkins Cove. "Where did you hear I'm staying at Drake House?"

"Shelley Zachary. You gave her something to gossip about, something besides Brandon's reasons for canceling the Christmas Ball." Lexie shook her head.

"You didn't tell me he was hurt when Charlotte died."

"I'm sorry, Marie. Your father asked me not to. He was afraid you'd come back. And I have to admit I agreed with him. The last time you were around Brandon, things didn't turn out so well. Be careful, won't you?"

Marie nodded, but she could tell by Lexie's expression that her friend wasn't convinced. "I'm just staying there to see if I can find some kind of evidence my father was murdered."

"That's another reason you're thinking about going to this psychomanteum thing at Sophie Caldwell's, aren't you? You want to ask about his death."

Marie nodded. She'd told Lexie her suspicions the morning before her father's funeral. Now after hearing what the medical examiner had to say, she felt she was on the right track. If she could learn something from the psychomanteum, anything at all, it would be worth it. "What do you think of the idea?"

Lexie shrugged. "Try it. What's to lose?"

"Will you come with me?"

Lexie shifted her work boots on the floor. "To hold your hand?" It was meant as a quip, but judging from Lexie's discomfort, she knew what Marie was about to say next.

"To contact Simon."

Lexie started shaking her head before the words were out of Marie's mouth. "Simon died thirteen years ago, Marie. There's no use trying to relive the past."

"Why not? Like you said, it might not work, but there's nothing to lose."

"There's nothing to gain, either. Simon's dead. Let's just leave it that way."

Marie nodded. She didn't want to press her friend. Lexie had gone through enough after Simon had died on that Christmas Eve they had planned to run away together. She'd raised his daughter alone. She'd thrown herself into her family's business. She'd pulled her life together. The last thing Marie wanted to do was make her feel as though she had to revisit those dark times. "You're right. You've moved on. You've done an amazing job with Katie."

Lexie pressed her lips into a smile. "Thanks. Although you might not agree when you meet her. She's got a pretty good preteen snit going on these days."

"I hear her mother and her mother's friend were pretty good at that preteen snit in their day."

Lexie smiled. "My mom always told me she hoped I had a daughter like me. Now she reminds me of that regularly."

At the mention of Lexie's mom, the tears misted Marie's eyes. She was all alone now. Now she didn't even have her dad. "I want to see your parents before I go back to Michigan."

"They would have your hide if you didn't." Lexie laid a hand on Marie's shoulder. "But now why don't you go ahead and try to contact your father? I have to deliver these wreaths to a client who lives near the harbor. I'll drive you to Sophie Caldwell's place."

MARIE FOLLOWED SOPHIE up the staircase to the third floor of the old bed-and-breakfast. She'd been chattering nonstop since Marie and Lexie had shown up at the door. Fine with Marie. The more Sophie talked, the less Marie had to. And right now she was so nervous, she doubted she could string three words together that made sense.

"The best way to do this is to spend a day meditating and centering yourself, honey. But nowadays, I know people just don't seem to have the time."

Unease fluttered in Marie's chest. "No. No time."

"I know you think I'm a little crazy with all this stuff, but you don't have to believe in ghosts, if you don't want to. Think of this as meditating. Just relax and open yourself to your deepest thoughts. That's all you need to do."

All? Right now she felt as though relaxing was the

toughest thing in the world, and she was trying to avoid her deepest thoughts.

"I use breathing exercises. In through the nose, out through the mouth. Count slowly while you're doing it. It calms me." Sophie reached the hallway at the top of the steps and spun to face Marie. She breathed in and out, moving her arms with each breath as if conducting an orchestra. She kept it up until Marie joined in. "That's it, sweetheart. In and out. In and out. Starting to feel better?"

"Strangely enough, I am."

"Good. Now follow me." Sophie pushed through a door and led Marie into a darkened room. She flicked a light switch.

Even with the overhead light blazing, the room still felt dark. Black-curtained walls, black ceiling and dark carpet made the space feel smaller than it probably was. Marie eyed the single chair positioned in the room's center. It faced a large gold-framed mirror. "That's the oracle."

"That's right."

Even though she knew the mirror was merely silvered glass, it felt deeper, as if it were calling to her, drawing her in.

She pulled her gaze away and scanned the rest of the items in the space. Antique chests and small tables dotted the carpet, the surface of each one covered with equally antique candelabra holding tapers and other holders cradling fat column candles.

"You built this place?"

"With the help of my handyman, Phil. Phil Cardon. I'm determined, but not exactly strong. Not physically strong, anyway." She pulled a long lighter from one of the tables and bustling around the room, she lit the candles. Once she'd finished, she snapped off the overhead switch. A gentle, flickering light filled the room. "I made my own candles, too. Sometimes scent is part of the experience we get from the other side. Perfumed candles can mask that. So all these are one hundred percent fragrance free."

Marie thought of the jasmine she'd smelled in Drake House. Maybe she was right to think of ghosts when she'd experienced that scent. Not that Brandon would agree.

Pressure assaulted her chest at the thought of him.

She pressed her hand against her breastbone and looked into the mirror. Her emotions were so jumbled where Brandon was concerned. That was part of why she was here. The part Lexie had guessed.

Her father loved Brandon like a son, yet he'd warned Marie about him ten years ago. About his need to be in control of his emotions. About his choice to marry Charlotte. Marie's father had helped her break her ties with Brandon and start a new life. She needed him to help her sort through her feelings now. "I sit in the chair, right?"

"That's right, dear. Look into the mirror and relax. Use those breathing exercises."

"How long will it take?"

"There's no telling. Sometimes communication happens right away. Sometimes it can take hours to open yourself up enough."

Marie lowered herself into the chair. Hours. She couldn't see herself staring into a mirror for hours. She didn't even like looking at her face for the five minutes it took to put on makeup in the morning. "I hope it's faster than that."

"You have to be patient." She could hear Sophie rustle toward the door behind her. "Concentrate on your father. How much you love him. How much you miss him." The woman's voice faltered. Clearly she was talking about her own feelings as much as Marie's.

Before Marie could turn around, the door closed, and she could hear Sophie's footsteps receding down the stairs.

Marie turned back to the mirror and looked into her own eyes. Tears sparkled at their corners in the candle-light. She did love her father. She did miss him. She ached at the prospect that she'd never again see his smile.

She scrutinized her own smile in the mirror. She wasn't ugly, but she was a far cry from the glamorous Charlotte. She didn't need a picture to remember Charlotte's wavy blond hair and flawless skin, her vibrant laugh, her sparkling, intelligent eyes. That was the woman Brandon had chosen. And that was the image she should keep in her mind, especially after what had happened today.

Or *almost* happened.

She let her eyes stare and become unfocused. Relax. That was what Sophie had said. Drift. Her image blurred, obscured by clouds of light and dark. This was better. At least now she didn't have to stare at herself, compare herself to Charlotte. She could just drift…open herself…love her father….

At first she didn't identify the scent. Exotic. Slightly spicy. Pleasant.

She pulled in a deep breath. It was that jasmine blend, all right. The same scent she had followed through the halls of Drake House. Charlotte's scent. She breathed in again, but the scent was gone.

She shifted in the chair.

"Marie." The voice was light as air.

Had Sophie returned? Marie twisted to look behind her.

The door was closed, the room empty.

"Murder." The voice again. The same one she'd heard in the radio static. Or was it?

A tremor seized Marie's chest.

"Murder."

There it was again, faint, indistinct. Marie could swear the sound was coming from the mirror, yet it was all over the room at the same time. "Daddy?" Even as she called out, she knew the whisper wasn't his. She stared at the center of the gold frame, waiting to see something, anything. But only her own reflection stared back. Candlelight danced behind her. "Who's there?"

The scent tickled her senses again. Jasmine.

"Charlotte? Is that you?"

The scent grew stronger.

This was crazy. It couldn't be happening. She must have fallen asleep in her chair. She must be dreaming.

Cold moved over her. Penetrating deep like the first cut of a blade. She gripped her legs and dug fingertips into the muscles of her thighs. "Charlotte? If it's you, answer."

"Marie." The voice hissed like a steam radiator. The scent grew overpowering.

Marie forced herself to stay in the chair, though every cell in her body clamored to run. "Charlotte? What is it? Why are you communicating with me?"

"Love." The hiss trailed off, but the word was clear.

Charlotte loved her? She found that impossible to believe. "You love Brandon. That's why you're speaking to me?"

"Love."

"Are you trying to warn me away from Brandon? Is that it? Are you staking your claim to him even from the grave?" Marie's inside shook. With fear, with anger, she wasn't sure which. She was getting tired of playing this guessing game. She wanted answers, and she wanted them now. "Out with it, Charlotte. What are you trying to say?"

The cold deepened. The tremor inside her grew until her whole body shook.

The hiss came again, barely loud enough to hear. "All Brandon loves will die."

Chapter Seven

Marie was still shaking when she arrived at the Jenkins Cove Police Station, only a few blocks from the B&B. After she heard the voice, she'd panicked, bolting out of the attic room. She'd escaped from the House of the Seven Gables without explaining to Sophie anything of what she'd experienced. What was she going to say? That Charlotte's ghost had spoken to her? That Charlotte said she was murdered? That the entity had suggested Brandon was responsible?

All Brandon loves will die.

Charlotte's ghost hadn't come out and said Brandon was responsible, only that those he loved would die. But what did that mean? That Charlotte's ghost would kill anyone Brandon loved? Was she warning Marie away?

Marie gathered her wool coat tight at the neck with one hand and clutched her bag against her side with the other. She didn't know what to believe. Heck, she didn't even know what she'd just experienced. But one thing was clear. She needed to know more about Charlotte's death. And save asking Brandon, the only place she could think to get that kind of information was the Jenkins Cove Police Station.

She set her jaw and mounted the steps of the remodeled old house that served as home to the police department. She wasn't sure how she was going to explain her questions to Chief Hammer. He'd probably think she was some kind of paranoid conspiracy nut, seeing a murder behind every accident.

She'd be happy if paranoia was all it was.

She stepped into the entry. Still sporting its original hardwood floors, the station looked very little like a house on the inside. Instead of a foyer, a high desk squatted about ten feet from the door, making it impossible to get into the rest of the station without being seen. A heavy woman wearing a trim polo shirt emblazoned with the Jenkins Cove PD seal looked up from the bank of three computer screens surrounding her. "Can I help you?"

"I was wondering if I could talk to someone about an accident investigation."

"Miss Leonard." Chief Hammer's voice vibrated off the hardwood floors. He poked his head around a corner and gave her an insincere smile. "Are you still *investigating* your father's death?"

She couldn't help note his patronizing tone. "Yes, I'm still looking for answers. But that's not why I'm here this afternoon. I was wondering if you could answer some questions I have about another matter."

Chief Hammer looked relieved. He actually gave her a friendly smile. "Come on in, then. We're pretty short-handed around here, but I'll see what I can do."

He led her into a surprisingly large office just around the corner from the dispatcher. "Have a seat."

Marie sat, though she'd rather stand. At least she remembered her manners this time. No reason to get the chief defensive about her refusing his offer of a chair before their chat even began. "I was wondering if you could fill me in on another accident that took place at Drake House in the past year."

His relieved look melted like an early snow. "Charlotte Drake."

"Yes."

He groaned and shook his head. "A horrible, tragic accident. But I'm not sure what you expect from me. If you want to know more about Mrs. Drake's accident, why don't you ask Brandon Drake himself? I hear you're staying out at Drake House."

It seemed the entire town knew she was staying at Drake House. Of course, Chief Hammer had learned of it from last night's break-in, not Shelley's gossip. "Brandon is still grieving. I don't want to upset him if I can help it." At least that was the truth.

"Of course." The chief leaned back in his desk chair and tented his fingers. "I'll do my best to answer, within reason. What do you want to know?"

"What happened that night?"

"Charlotte, er, Mrs. Drake was drinking. Late in the evening she got into her car. She lost control, and her car collided with a stone wall on the property. The gas tank ruptured, and the fuel ignited."

"And Brandon?"

"Oh yes. Brandon was badly burned trying to pull her out of the fire."

Marie loosened her grip on her coat. She set her bag in the chair beside her. Brandon had risked his life to save Charlotte. So he couldn't have been responsible, could he?

Murder.

The word popped into Marie's mind, carried on a whisper as it had been in the psychomanteum and on the radio. If not Brandon, could someone else have killed Charlotte? "Was there any evidence of foul play?"

There was the expression she knew was coming. The expression that said Chief Hammer thought she was out of her ever-loving mind. "You're kidding, right?" He glanced around his office as if Marie were setting him up, and he was searching for the camera that must be recording the joke.

"No. I'm not kidding. I'm asking. Was there any chance Charlotte's death wasn't completely accidental?"

His gaze finally landed back on her. "It was an accident, Miss Leonard. Just like your father's death was an accident. Neither of them was murdered."

"I can understand why it seems far-fetched for Drake House to see two unrelated murders in the span of six months, Chief. But two accidents in that time span seems odd, too." She paused, weighing her words, careful not to offend Chief Hammer. "What if my father found out something about Charlotte's death? What if he was murdered to keep him quiet?"

A bushy brow crooked toward his nonexistent hairline. "Are you sure you're not some kind of murder-mystery writer?"

"I'm serious, Chief."

"I'm serious, too, Miss Leonard. I don't know what you're after here, but this is ridiculous. And it's starting to get on my nerves. We're very busy around here with real life. I don't need to spend any more of my time on your silly theories."

Obviously she had no talent for diplomacy. "Really, if you hear me—"

"I'm done here, Miss Leonard." Hammer rose to his full modest height. "If there's anything rational that we can do for you here at the police department, let us know."

"Would it be possible for me to see Charlotte Drake's accident report?"

"Why would you want to do that?"

"I need to understand what happened."

Hammer puffed out his bulldog cheeks. He didn't move.

"Accident reports are public record, aren't they?"

With a grunt, he thrust himself from his chair and stalked to the office door. "I'll get them for you. It might take a while. Half my staff is assisting the state police." He closed the door behind him, leaving her alone in the office.

Time ticked by, and Hammer didn't return. Finally Marie left the office to find out what had happened to the chief and his promise. Rounding the corner, she stepped into the dispatch area.

The last person she expected to see was Brandon. But there he was, powerfully sexy in his black leather coat, taking a sheaf of papers from the chief himself. "Hello, Marie."

"Chief Hammer called you, didn't he?" Marie stopped stock-still on the police station's front porch and stared a hole through Brandon.

Brandon's gut ached. "What does it matter? You needed a ride back to Drake House, anyway." He looked out across the street where his car idled, Josef waiting patiently for them. Clouds hung low and ominous in the sky. The air smelled like coming rain.

"You could have waited until I called. You could have sent the car. Why did he call you? Because I was asking too many questions?"

"Because you were forcing him to work too hard, I think."

Marie and he had found common ground when he'd mentioned Hammer's laziness last night. Now her expression darkened and she clamped her jaw tight. "What did he say to you? Be honest."

Brandon should have known Marie wouldn't let him get away with ducking the subject. He used to like that about her. Her directness. Her doggedness. Now he wasn't so sure. "He said you were asking a lot of questions about Charlotte. Questions he thought I could do a better job of answering."

"Or a better job of avoiding?"

She was right. The last thing he wanted to do was stand here in the rain and talk about Charlotte. Especially with her.

"You rushed over here to get me to back off, didn't you?"

"Yes."

"You don't want to talk about Charlotte."

"No."

Her lips tightened. She clutched the top of her coat, pulling it protectively around her throat.

"What do you expect me to do? Lie? I don't want to relive Charlotte's death, especially not with you." He gripped the head of his cane until his fingers ached. His wedding band dug into his flesh. Having Marie around had been a struggle from the first moment. Between his old feelings for her coming to life and his need to keep from hurting her again, he'd tied himself in knots. But he really couldn't stomach dredging up his past with Charlotte. His failure. His guilt. Scars so much deeper than the ones on his face and leg. "Why are you asking about Charlotte? What could you possibly need to know?"

"I think she was murdered."

He took a step backward, his heel hitting the base of the porch railing. He'd been ready for her to say a lot of things, but not that. "Why on earth would you think she was murdered?"

She rolled her lower lip inward and grasped it in her teeth. "Something Sophie Caldwell said."

"What?"

"She said my father discovered something right before he died. Something he told her was dangerous."

"Why do you think whatever it was he found has anything to do with Charlotte's death?"

She searched his eyes, her gaze moving back and forth as if she wasn't finding what she was looking for. "Doesn't it seem strange to you? I mean, two fatal accidents at Drake House in a six month time period?"

"I already told you I agree your father's death seems suspicious."

"Then an accident and a murder."

"Coincidences can happen."

She stiffened and shook her head. "You're not listening."

"No, you're not listening, Marie. I *know* Charlotte wasn't murdered. I know why she died. I was there, remember?"

She released her coat and balled her fists at her sides, her chest rising and falling with shaky breaths. "No, I don't remember. You haven't told me anything about

Charlotte's death. Neither did Chief Hammer. Neither did my father or Lexie. Everyone seems to be trying to protect me. Well, I don't need protection. And I don't want it. I want the truth. I want some answers."

"Charlotte wasn't murdered."

She held up a hand as if shielding herself from his words. "*I* have reason to believe she was. Not just what Sophie said, but reasons I don't want to talk about. *And* I have reason to believe my father was murdered after he found out who killed her. Probably by the same person."

He drew in a breath to speak.

Marie gestured again with her hand. Her fingers were trembling. "I don't want to hear your pronouncements. If you can't enlighten me, stay out of my way."

God, he hated to see her so upset. And he had no one to blame but himself. He had been avoiding the subject of Charlotte since her death. It was the reason he avoided venturing out into public wherever possible. It was the reason he canceled the Christmas Ball. It was the reason he discouraged the few servants he tolerated around him from even mentioning her name. He even tried to prevent himself from thinking about her, although he failed regularly at that. And since Marie had come back to Drake House…

He waved an arm, directing Josef to swing the car around to this side of the street. Brandon knew that he'd made a royal mess of everything, and that he needed to set things straight. To come clean. At least with Marie. The rest of the damage he'd done could never be repaired. "Marie? Get in the car and I'll tell you everything."

As Josef pulled to the curb, Brandon stepped off the

porch. Drizzle misted the car's windows and felt cool on his cheeks. He opened the back door and gestured Marie inside.

She held his eyes for a second, as if deciding whether he was sincere about his promise. Then she slid into the seat. He followed, settling in beside her. For a moment all he could think about was kissing her, actually going through with it this time and pressing his lips to hers. Tasting her mouth. Feeling her body yield to his, soft and accepting.

He nodded for Josef to drive and focused straight ahead. As they drove through town, he watched the windshield wipers sweep the glass periodically and searched for words that would make this easier.

Nothing would make it easier.

Finally he just spoke. "Charlotte lost control of her car. As she was leaving Drake House, she veered off the drive just before the gate and hit the rock wall. Her car caught fire. I heard the impact. I saw the fire. I tried to pull her out, but she was trapped in the wreckage. She died right in front of me. I heard her last screams." He kept his voice flat, unemotional, but his stomach seized involuntarily at the memory. Charlotte's screams were always in his nightmares. Always lurking in the back of his mind.

Marie shook her head. "A woman doesn't just race her car into a stone wall. A car doesn't just burst into flame."

"I was there. It did."

"Did you see her before it happened?"

The tension in his stomach turned to nausea. And he'd thought this couldn't get worse.

"You said you'd explain. You said you'd tell me everything."

He blew air through tight lips. "Yes, I did."

"So?"

"Yes, I saw her."

"Was she upset about anything? How did she seem? Chief Hammer said she was drinking."

"She was."

"Why?"

For a one word question, that one was about as complicated as a question could get. "She just did. She collected fine wine. I still have the wine cellar to prove it."

"So she always drank?"

"She liked her wine."

"Chief Hammer said there was a vodka bottle."

"Yes. The police found it in the car. He told me that after the accident."

"Did Charlotte drink a lot?"

He couldn't stand this. "I don't think this has anything to do with anything. Sure, she was drunk. Sure, she shouldn't have been behind the wheel."

"Then why was she? Josef could have driven her, couldn't he? Was he working for you then?"

"She could have had him drive her. Back then we used him more as a handyman than a driver. We usually drove ourselves." He looked down at his leg. Those days were over. Now he was lucky to be able to walk, albeit with a cane. His doctor doubted his reflexes would ever be sharp enough again to drive safely.

Marie shook her head. "Charlotte didn't strike me as the type of woman who would—"

"We had a fight, all right? She was upset with me. That's why she was drinking. That's why she got behind the wheel. That's why she crashed."

The click of the turn signal and the swoosh of the wipers were the only sounds as they approached the long, winding drive. The gray stone wall stretched along the highway, opening only for the classic white pillar entrance of Drake House and the ostentatious redbrick and cast iron of his uncle's neighboring estate, The Manor at Drake Acres. Josef slowed the car to make the turn.

Brandon stared straight out the window. He didn't want to witness Marie's reaction to his confession. Getting the words out had been hard enough. Nor could he bear to look out the side window and see the stone wall as they passed.

The wall that still held a shadow of fire.

"It's not your fault, Brandon." Her voice sounded calm, soothing, forgiving.

He shook his head. He couldn't let himself listen. It was enough to undo him. "You still don't understand. It *is* my fault. It's all my fault. Charlotte was a good wife. She was kind and beautiful and so damn smart. She was any man's dream. And what did I do to repay her?" He lowered his head and pinched the bridge of his nose between thumb and forefinger. He couldn't explain. Not to Marie. Never to Marie.

"You had an affair?"

"No!"

"What, then? What did you fight about?"

He promised he'd tell her everything. He promised he'd be honest with her. But how could he be honest about this?

"What did you fight about, Brandon? What was so bad?"

He clutched the head of his cane in both hands.

Avoiding the platinum gleam of the ring around his finger, he raised his eyes to meet hers.

Most men probably wouldn't find Marie as beautiful as Charlotte. But most men were fools. To him, one look into Marie's eyes was more addictive than any drug. It had always been that way. Ever since the summer when he'd come home with his MBA from Harvard and found her all grown up. And try as he might, he hadn't been able to change his response. He couldn't change his response to her even now. "Charlotte and I fought about you."

Chapter Eight

"Me?" The word caught in Marie's throat, almost choking her. She couldn't have heard Brandon right. How could they have fought about her? At the time of Charlotte's death, she hadn't seen either of them for ten years. "I don't understand."

"Of course you don't. You're strong, resilient. After that summer, you moved on."

"After that summer?" Marie's stomach tightened into a knot. There was no question what summer he meant. The summer she'd given him everything she was, and he'd tossed it away. "You make it seem as if moving on was my choice. As if I had a choice at all. After that summer, you got married."

The car's tires popped over loose gravel. Drake House loomed at the end of the winding drive, bright white columns glowing in the dreary weather, gray slate roof glistening with rain. The crunch of the tires slowed. The car stopped in front of the main entrance.

"You were so young, just out of high school. I already had my MBA. I was ready to settle down in Jenkins Cove and run the Drake Foundation. I couldn't tie you down when you hadn't even had a chance to see the world."

"That's what my father told you."

"And he was right. You deserved the chance to live your own life. To see the world beyond Jenkins Cove. To discover who you wanted to be." He lifted his hand. For a moment, he let it hover in the air, as if he wanted to touch her, before returning it to his cane. "It wasn't just that. I had already promised Charlotte. She was a good woman. My age. Already accomplished. Ready to settle down. I thought she was the perfect wife for me. I had no misgivings about marrying her. Not until…that summer with you. That summer made me rethink everything I thought I knew, everything I thought I felt. I didn't know what to trust—feelings that had swept me up in one summer or plans that were years in the making."

So he went with the plans.

Marie stared at the grand house. She didn't want to hear this. Any of it. She'd tried so hard to overcome her feelings for Brandon. She'd tried so hard to forget him and stand on her own. "Why are you telling me this?"

"You asked."

"I asked about Charlotte's death. Not about you and me."

"But it's all linked. It's all tangled into one giant mess."

She focused on Brandon. "How?"

He tore his eyes from hers. "Josef?"

The chauffeur glanced over his shoulder. "Yes, sir?"

"We would like some privacy. Just turn off the engine and leave the car here."

"Very good, sir." The chauffeur switched off the engine and left the keys dangling in the ignition. He climbed from the driver's seat and closed the door behind him, the sound followed by an abrupt and deep silence.

Marie watched him cut across the lawn to the carriage house. With each step he took away from the car, the more panicked she felt. She wanted to call the chauffeur back, ask him to stay, use him to shield her from whatever was coming. She didn't know what Brandon was going to say, but she had the feeling that whatever it was, it would be better for her not to hear.

"Charlotte deserved someone who loved her."

Marie let his words settle into her brain. She felt Brandon's pain in them, his regret. But the shift inside her was more insidious, more dangerous. It was the shift from numbness to hope.

And that scared her more than anything.

She clutched the bag in her lap and held on. She had to get a grip on herself. She was no longer eighteen. She had to remember all she'd learned.

Her father had warned her about Brandon that summer. He'd told her of Brandon's childhood. Of the heartbreak Brandon suffered when he'd lost his mother and the tightrope he'd had to walk to please his demanding father and grandfather. Her father feared Brandon had been damaged. He feared all the trauma he'd suffered as a boy had combined to make him afraid to open himself to love. To vulnerability.

Even with a woman as amazing as Charlotte.

And that's what she had to keep foremost in her mind. Her father's warning. Her father's fears. Not the way Brandon had looked at her that summer as if she were beautiful. Not his tenderness when they'd made love, when she'd given him her virginity. And certainly not the kiss he'd almost given her this morning, the kiss she still longed to claim.

"That night..." Brandon's voice cracked. He drew a

deep breath. "The night Charlotte died, she asked me for one thing. Something I couldn't give."

Marie wrapped her arms around her middle and held on. She needed to stay in control of her feelings, her fantasies. She didn't want to go back to that raw, painful place. The place it had taken her years to escape.

Brandon reached into his pocket and pulled out a leather wallet. He flipped it open and slipped something free. He handed Marie a small photograph.

She tilted it toward the car's window. Her high school graduation picture stared back at her, long hair, freckles, goofy smile and all. "My senior picture?"

"Charlotte found it the night she died. She asked me to get rid of it. I couldn't."

Marie looked up at him. She didn't want to know…she didn't want to ask…but she couldn't help it. "Why?"

"I don't know."

She closed her eyes. She'd dreamed for years that someday Brandon would tell her he loved her. That he'd made a mistake. That he wanted her instead of Charlotte. Now even though he'd admitted to arguing with his wife about her picture, he still wouldn't say those special words.

And the worst part of it all, the part that made her feel sick inside, was that she still wanted to hear them. "That's what you fought over? My picture?"

"Yes." He shook his head, the movement slow and sad. "I never should have asked Charlotte to marry me. It wasn't fair to her. But I didn't know that. Not until after I'd proposed. Not until that summer."

That summer. Their summer. Marie watched the drizzle bead up and slide down the window like tears.

Now that he'd put his regrets out there, she had to know the rest. "Why did you go through with the wedding?"

"I didn't know how to break it off. There were so many reasons not to. My promise to her. Our families. And she suited me. At least I thought she should. My feelings for you were so new. So overwhelming. I'd never experienced feelings like that before. I didn't trust them. And because I was weak and indecisive..." He pinched the bridge of his nose once more, as if he thought doing so would push back the tears. "And because I was weak and indecisive, Charlotte paid the price."

Marie wrapped her arms tighter. She felt cold. Colder even than the Michigan winter. Suddenly what he'd been trying to say about Charlotte's death dawned on her, what he'd been trying to tell her all along. "You think she committed suicide."

He looked past her, past Drake House. Pain etched his face. His eyes looked more flat and hopeless than the overcast sky.

She had to go on. She had to know. For so long she'd kept a glimmer of hope alive...the wish that she and Brandon would find a way to be together. She'd tended it like a flicker of fire in the hearth, but with his confession, Brandon had doused the flame. "You think she killed herself because of you. Because you couldn't love her the way she needed. Because of the feelings you had for me. That's why you feel so guilty. You blame yourself for her death."

He looked down at his hands, knuckles white, clutching the carved head of his cane. He didn't speak. He didn't nod. He didn't answer at all.

He didn't have to.

MARIE STOOD in the darkened foyer of Drake House and stared up at the majestic twin staircase. For the first time she could remember, she felt truly relieved to be away from Brandon. After disabling the alarm and instructing her to lock the door behind him, he'd said something about wanting to check the boathouse. Promising to be back soon, he'd left her in the house alone.

Understandable that he wanted to be alone with his thoughts. With his regrets. She wanted to be alone, too, but not to think. She would be just fine if she never had to think of this evening again.

She mounted the steps. When she reached the first landing where the staircase split, each branch leading into opposite wings of the mansion, she paused. To the right, the stairs climbed into the house's grand ballroom and outer sitting rooms. Usually this time of year, the wing would be humming with activity as servants and outside contractors like Lexie readied it for the annual Drake House Christmas Ball. It would smell of pine boughs and cinnamon and jingle with music. Instead the space felt vacant and dead. No festive decor. No bustling energy. Just a forlorn sadness that made Marie miss her childhood Christmases even more.

But she wasn't here to relive Christmas memories and mourn the demise of Drake House tradition.

She turned away from the public west wing and started up the stairs that led east. She wasn't sure how Brandon would feel about her snooping in the house's private wing. Especially after what he'd just confessed. But just in case he didn't like the idea, she wasn't going to wait to ask permission. Better to ask forgiveness, as the saying went. Better still to find some evidence of murder—either Charlotte's or her father's. Then she wouldn't have to ask for anything.

Climbing the steps, Marie moved out of the light of the foyer and into the dark, enclosed portion of the staircase that led up to the rooms on the third floor. She groped along the wall. She had no idea where the light switches for the stairs and halls were located in this wing. She had only been in this area of the house a few times when she was young. The last time she'd ventured this way, she'd been exploring the house with Lexie. When her father had discovered them in the private wing unaccompanied and without permission, he'd grounded her for a week and called Lexie's parents. After that, they'd confined their exploring to the ballroom, parlors and guest quarters of the public wing.

She gripped the banister, feeling jittery in the dark, as if her father were going to jump out at any moment and demand to know why she was there. She smiled at the thought. She wouldn't mind being grounded for a week if she could see his face once more. She wouldn't mind at all.

Reaching the third floor, she stopped and tried to get her bearings. The rain sounded as if it was coming down harder now, its patter a constant din on the roof a full floor above her head. Located on a jut of land, Drake House offered views of the water on three sides. She peered through an open door facing the forest side of the house. The nursery. Big enough to house half a dozen children, it stood empty now, the whimsical carving of animals along the ceiling molding merely a reminder of the next generation of Drake children who would never occupy this space. She passed several locked doors she remembered were the nanny's quarters and various other rooms before reaching the back staircase that led to the third floor.

If she remembered correctly, Charlotte's study overlooked the east garden, which would put it at the end of the wing. When her father was first working up plans with Lexie for redesigning the garden's landscaping, he'd mentioned how enthusiastic Charlotte had been, since her rooms overlooked that part of the property.

Unfortunately, she'd died before work on the garden began.

Marie forced her feet to move down the dark hall. A door facing the water side of the house stood open. Despite a shimmer of unease at the back of her neck, she stopped in front of an open door and peered inside.

The wet glisten of rain and water shone through windows unencumbered by draperies. Heavy, masculine chairs clustered in the sitting area. The scent of leather hung rich in the air. She stepped farther into the room, to the next open door and the chamber beyond. A bed big enough for five people faced a window overlooking Chesapeake Bay.

The master bedroom suite.

Marie's pulse pounded in her ears. It didn't take much imagination to see Brandon in that bed, leaning back against the pillows, his bare chest gleaming in the first glow of the morning sun.

She shook her head. Blocking the image in her mind's eye, she returned to the hall. She felt like that girl again, exploring places she shouldn't, indulging in feelings she had no business feeling. She needed to forget what she and Brandon had together all those years ago. Forget the hurt. Forget it all.

Hearing Charlotte's voice and smelling her scent in the psychomanteum might or might not qualify her as insane, but going through the same thing over and over with Brandon and expecting a different outcome was the *definition* of insanity. She needed to wipe Brandon from her mind...and her heart.

Swallowing into a dry throat, she walked farther down the hall. She passed the open entrance to Brandon's study and skipped the door she knew led up to the widow's walk on the roof. At the eastern-most end of the wing, she stopped at a locked door and pulled the ring of keys from her bag. Trying each, she finally found the one that fit. She let herself in and flicked on the light.

Lamps artfully positioned around the room gave off a soft glow. The room was as feminine as the master suite was masculine. Dainty antique chairs covered with silk damask gathered around a fireplace. Built-in bookshelves flanked an ornate antique desk. Pillows decorated a floral sofa. And the scent...jasmine.

She drew in a deep, slow breath. Sure enough. The same scent she'd noticed last night. The same one she'd smelled in the psychomanteum. This wasn't her imagination. She wasn't crazy. This was real.

Like last night, she let the scent lead her across the study, toward the windows and the desk positioned underneath.

If Charlotte's spirit was responsible for the scent of jasmine and the voice she'd heard in the psychomanteum, maybe she was trying to tell Marie something now. "Charlotte? Are you here?"

There was no reply.

"Is there something to find here?"

Again, silence answered.

Great. Now she was talking to herself. At least there was no one home to hear. She could just imagine how Brandon would feel about her wandering through the house calling out his dead wife's name. "Charlotte, if that's you, did you commit suicide?"

A sharp thud came from somewhere in the house.

Marie jumped. Was that an answer? Or was the wind kicking up outside? "If that was you, Charlotte, it wasn't clear enough. You talked to me in the psychomanteum. Why not talk to me now?"

No sound. Just the scent.

Marie eyed the antique desk under the window. "Is it the desk? Is there something inside?" She didn't wait for a response this time. She pulled open the top drawer.

Empty. The second was empty as well, and the third. She moved to the closet, then on to the built-in wall units. There was nothing to be found. Brandon might have left the furniture in the room, but he'd cleaned out all Charlotte's personal things. Marie wondered what he'd done with them.

A creak sounded from the hallway. The soft, slow beat of footsteps.

Brandon.

Marie turned away from the empty wall units and walked to the door, her skin prickling with nerves. She told herself she was being ridiculous. There was no reason to sneak around, no reason to hide what she'd been doing. If Brandon didn't want her looking through the house, he wouldn't have given her the full set of keys. Still, the thought of facing him again after what he'd revealed in the car left her a little shaky.

No matter. She wasn't going to hide from him the rest of her time in Jenkins Cove. She needed answers, starting with what had happened to Charlotte's personal papers and possessions. She was going to get to the bottom of Charlotte's and her father's deaths, and she wasn't going to let anything get in the way. Especially not the past.

She crossed the room and opened the door. The hall was dark, and for a moment all she could see was a shadow.

A shadow without a cane. A shadow too short to be Brandon.

Suddenly the shadow rushed toward her and an arm clamped around her throat.

Chapter Nine

Rain spattered cold on Marie's cheeks. She could feel hands gripping her under her arms, pulling her. Her feet dragged over something rough.

She must have passed out.

She remembered the shadow, remembered the arm across her throat, bearing down. Her head throbbed. Her stomach swirled. Her throat burned like fire.

But she could breathe.

She scooped in breath after breath of cold, moist air and tried to fight her way to consciousness. She tensed her muscles. She forced her eyes open.

Color exploded in her head. Her vision swirled, dark and light. The night closed in around her. She saw the water far below, and white lines stretching on either side of her. They were the rails encircling the widow's walk.

She was on the roof.

She gritted her teeth and tried to clear her head, tried to think. Hell, she didn't have time to think. She had to move. She thrust her arms up, lashing out at the hands dragging her. She bared her fingernails like claws, trying to dig her stubby nails into flesh.

A blow rained down on her head, and rough hands pushed her into the railing. The top rail hit low on her thighs, but her upper body kept moving, flipping, carrying her over.

She hit the sloped roof. Air exploded from her lungs. She coughed, gasped, tried to breathe. Her body started to slide.

She scrambled to find a handhold, a foothold, but wet with rain, the shingles felt slick as ice. Her fingers slipped. Her feet thrashed.

And still she kept sliding. Closer to the edge. Closer to the three-story drop to the ground.

Her hand hit something. A roof vent. She grabbed on, the steel cutting into her fingers. Her legs jutted out over the roof's edge.

She stopped.

She clung to the vent, afraid to move. Rain pattered on her back. Water sluiced around her, beneath her and emptied into the gutter that ran under her legs. Her heart pounded against the wet slate. She slowly, carefully scooped in a breath. Then another. Her lungs screamed for more.

She peered down, past her dangling legs. She could see the gentle lighting of the east garden through the misty rain below. The concrete bench glowed pale against dark leaves of holly. So far down...so far...

She grew dizzy and closed her eyes. The edge of metal cut into her fingers. Her muscles trembled and ached. Her fingers started slipping.

Oh God. She was going to fall.

Pressure closed around her wrist and held her fast. Not cold like the rain, like the slate and steel she clung to, but warm as a human hand.

She looked up into the night. Through the rain the widow's walk railing gleamed white against a black sky. She was alone. Totally alone. And yet she could feel a hand on her wrist, a hand that kept her from falling, a hand that kept her safe.

"Marie?" a woman's voice screamed. Not from the roof, but from below. "Oh God, Marie! Hold on! We'll be right up."

Marie didn't know how long she clung there, the unseen hand binding her wrist, before she heard a clatter on the roof.

"Over here. This is where I saw her." A thump came from above. "We're here, Marie. We're coming for you."

The same woman's voice. A voice Marie recognized. "Chelsea?" What was Sophie Caldwell's niece doing here?

"Hold on, Marie."

Something scraped against the slate shingles above her head. A large hand encircled her wrist, replacing the pressure that had stopped her fall. "I've got you."

She looked up into a man's eyes. Rain sparkled in his dark hair. He gave her a reassuring smile. "It's okay. You can let go now."

She forced her fingers to obey.

He pulled her up, slowly, gently, until the two of them reached Chelsea on the widow's walk.

"Thank God," Chelsea said. "It's a miracle you held on. It took a few minutes to rig a rope. We were afraid you'd fall before Michael could reach you."

And she might have.

Marie looked out over the wet slate. Her whole body trembled. Her legs felt like loose sand. "Something held me. A hand. It kept me from going over the edge, but I couldn't see anything there. It was like…" She searched for the word, but her mind balked. Even after the experiences she'd had lately, she didn't want to say it out loud.

Michael gave a knowing nod. "A spirit?"

"Yes."

Chelsea and Michael exchanged looks. "Let's go inside," Chelsea said. "We have a lot to talk about."

WHEN BRANDON MOUNTED the steps to the kitchen entrance of Drake House he was surprised to see the lights still on in Edwin's quarters. He'd sat in the boathouse for hours and listened to the rain patter on the roof, trying to process what had happened with Marie, trying to get his head straight. And even though he didn't feel any better than he had when he'd left, he thought by now it would be safe to return to the house. He thought she would be asleep.

He unlocked the kitchen door and stepped inside. The door to the butler's quarters stood open. "Let me check your eyes again, just to be sure." A woman's voice. Not Marie.

He crossed the kitchen and peered through the open door.

A blond woman leaned over Marie's chair. She directed a flashlight to the side of Marie's cheek and peered into Marie's eyes, one after another. "Looks good. I think you're going to survive."

Alarm prickled along Brandon's nerves. He stepped forward into Edwin's sitting room. "Survive? Survive what?"

"You must be Brandon." A man nearly as tall as

Brandon with the build of an athlete pushed himself up from a chair. He stepped across the room and offered his hand. "Michael Bryant. This is Chelsea Caldwell."

Brandon made the connections in his mind while shaking the man's hand. He nodded to the blonde. "You're related to Sophie Caldwell?"

"My aunt."

So they'd made their introductions, but no one had answered his initial question. He focused on Marie. "What happened, Marie? Are you hurt?"

Marie wrapped her arms around herself as if she was cold. She looked so small sitting on the love seat. Small and fragile.

"Marie had an accident," the blonde supplied.

Something inside him seized. He struggled to keep himself steady, to stay calm and wait for the details instead of racing to Marie and gathering her into his arms. "What kind of accident?"

Marie glanced from Chelsea to Michael. "Thanks so much for everything you've done. And everything you told me. I think it's better if I talk to Brandon alone, if you don't mind."

"Yes. That's a good idea." Chelsea exchanged looks with Michael. Brandon led them to the front entrance of Drake House. "Thank you," he said as they plunged out into the rain and ran to their vehicle. Brandon locked the door and set the alarm behind them.

When he walked back into Edwin's sitting room, Marie was still huddled on the love seat. She looked as if she hadn't moved a muscle. A welt rose on her scalp, just above her right ear.

"You're hurt."

"Just a bump and a headache. I don't have a concussion. Believe me, Chelsea has been checking me every hour. I guess I just have a hard head."

His gaze moved down to her neck. Although she had a throw blanket wrapped around her shoulders, he could see a bruise starting to purple on the pale skin of her throat. He swayed a little on his feet. "And that?"

"I'll tell you about all of it. But first, you'd better sit down."

Brandon didn't move. "Who did this? Have you called the police?"

"They were already here."

"And a doctor? You need to see a doctor. We need to get you to a hospital. I'll call Josef."

"A paramedic was here, too. I'm just bruised. I'm going to be fine. Now sit down."

He couldn't. He needed to do something. Sitting felt too passive. Besides, the only place he wanted to sit was in the love seat beside her. More than anything he wanted to take her in his arms and keep her safe. "I'll stand."

"Fine." She explained how she'd been looking through Charlotte's study, how she'd thought she'd heard him return from the boathouse, how she'd been attacked. When she got to the part about being thrown off the roof, he started pacing, a habit he'd broken since he'd injured his leg. A habit that saved him now. "Why didn't I hear any of this? I should have heard something. I should have known. You could have died." Damn him. Marie had already been attacked once since she came to Drake House. Why in the hell had he left her alone? What had he been thinking?

"Chelsea found me. She and Michael saved me."

He managed a nod. What he wanted to do was smack himself in the head…or worse.

He ran a hand through his hair before walking back the length of the room. He hadn't been thinking. Not about anyone but himself, anyway. He'd simply wanted to get away. Far away. Where he didn't have to see the pain and disappointment in Marie's eyes. Where he wouldn't be tempted to take her in his arms and make promises he feared he could never keep.

At least Chelsea Caldwell and this Michael had been here. Brandon eyed Marie. "Why *were* Chelsea and Michael here? And how did they find you on the roof?"

"Chelsea sensed I was in trouble."

"She *sensed* it?"

"She sees things other people don't see."

"Like what? The future?"

Marie watched him. A little too closely for his comfort. "She sees ghosts. They communicate with her."

His stomach felt as if he were cresting in a roller coaster and hanging in midair. "You're joking."

"You know the mass grave we've been hearing so much about? Do you know how the police discovered it?"

She'd lost him. "What does the mass grave have to do with what happened tonight?"

"A spirit named Lavinia appeared to Chelsea. Michael saw her, too. The spirit led them to the graves. She helped them figure out the truth."

"Let me guess, Lavinia was one of the people buried in the mass grave."

"Yes."

He massaged his forehead with his fingertips. What kinds of stories had Chelsea and Michael been telling? "You don't believe all this stuff, do you?"

Marie watched him a long time. Rain and wind beat against the windows and whistled over the chimneys of the old house. He was about to ask again when Marie finally spoke. "Yes. I do."

"You're kidding."

She narrowed her eyes to caramel-colored slits. "You don't believe there are things in this world that we don't understand?"

"Things like ghosts?" He couldn't even believe they were having this conversation, and he still had no clue where it was leading. "I've never really thought about it."

"Would you believe if you saw one? Or heard one?"

"I don't know. I suppose I might."

"Would you believe if I told you that a ghost has contacted me?"

An uneasy feeling knotted deep in his gut. "How did this go from a story Chelsea told you to this? What are you trying to say, Marie?"

"Just that. I've been contacted by a spirit. I didn't want to believe it myself at first. But it's real."

He shook his head.

Marie slumped back in the love seat. "You don't believe me. You haven't even heard what I have to say, and you don't believe me."

"I'm just trying to get this straight." He didn't have a clue what to think. This whole conversation was so unlike Marie. She had a romantic streak, yes. But she always seemed to have her feet firmly planted in reality. She was like her father in that way. "The ghost you saw. It was your father?"

"I didn't *see* a ghost. I heard a voice. I smelled a scent."

He went cold inside. Memories of their argument at the police station popped into his mind. The way Marie had insisted Charlotte had been murdered. She couldn't be leading where he feared she was. She wouldn't. "It was your father, right?" *Please let it be Edwin.*

"I tried to contact my father. I couldn't reach him."

"Then…" He couldn't ask. He didn't want to know.

"Brandon, it was Charlotte."

"The jasmine."

"Exactly."

"It was a scent, Marie. Just a scent. Charlotte lived here for ten years. It isn't unheard of that the house would still smell like her."

"I didn't just smell it here. I smelled it in Sophie's psychomanteum."

"How do you know the scent was Charlotte? How do you know it wasn't from some other source? Jasmine isn't common, but it's not rare, either."

"I heard her voice, Brandon."

His heart stuttered. "You're sure?"

"Yes."

Even though he had an idea of what Marie's answer would be, he forced the question from his lips. "What did she say?"

"She said she was murdered. She said, 'All Brandon loves will die.'"

He stared at the wall, the moldings on the ceiling, anything but Marie. The part about Charlotte saying she was murdered, he'd guessed. The other part…*All Brandon loves will die.* What did that mean?

"You still don't believe." Marie's voice trembled.

Something inside him broke at the sound. He met her eyes. "It's not that I don't want to, Marie. I just…"

"You can't."

"I don't know. I'm trying to absorb it. That's all." He turned away from her and strode the length of the room, the extra beat of his cane on the parquet making his footfalls sound as unbalanced as all of this felt.

Murder. Charlotte murdered. As much as he wanted to believe Marie, as much as he wanted to believe Charlotte hadn't killed herself, that he wasn't responsible for his wife's death, he didn't know if he could. "Who would murder Charlotte?"

"You tell me. Did anyone stand to gain from her death?"

"You mean financially?"

"Sure. Or other ways."

He walked back to where Marie sat. The answer to her question was obvious and inevitable. "Me."

Marie shook her head. "Who else?"

"No one else." He thought for a moment. This whole exercise was so foreign to him. Murder? Motives? For crying out loud, *ghosts?* It was as if he'd fallen down some surreal rabbit hole. "Her mother is still alive. But she isn't in need of money. And she adored her daughter. She was crushed when Charlotte died."

Marie stared into the empty fireplace, deep in thought. "What if you died without having children? Who would inherit?"

"My uncle. He's not in need of money, either." Brandon took several steps and stopped. The words Marie had repeated, the ones she said had come from the ghost, whispered through his mind.

All Brandon loves will die.

His fingers tightened on his cane. Charlotte had died, only he hadn't loved Charlotte. Not the way a man should love his wife. But… "What about this attack tonight?"

She met his eyes, unflinching. "I'm pretty sure my father was killed because he found something, something that proved Charlotte was murdered. Maybe the killer thinks I've found whatever that is. Or maybe he or she is afraid I will."

There was one other possibility. One Brandon didn't want to entertain. That a ghost's warning was real. The ghost of his dead wife.

He finished his trek back to the love seat.

Arms wrapped around herself, Marie peered up at him, so pale, so fragile. Even though he knew she was strong as steel inside, he still had the urge to sweep her into his arms and take her far away. Somewhere she would be safe.

He wasn't sure he could believe any of this. But maybe he didn't have to. Maybe his role was simpler than that. "I don't know what's real and what's not, Marie. But I know one thing. Whoever attacked you tonight, I won't let him hurt you again. I promise you that."

Chapter Ten

Marie had heard all about the ostentatious redbrick mansion Clifford Drake had built on the jut of Drake family land right across the small inlet from Drake House. She'd even seen it across the water. But none of that was the same as having it looming before her now, up close and personal.

Josef held the car door. Brandon climbed out and joined Marie on the sidewalk. "Here it is. The Manor at Drake Acres. Uncle Cliff's answer to the fact that my father inherited Drake House."

"It sure is big." And red. The rich color of the brick glowed in the morning sun. His tall white pillars and three and a half stories' worth of windows stretched up to the gabled roof.

"Big. Yes. I think that's what he was going for. Bigger than Drake House, at any rate."

Marie had to turn her head first fully to one side, then to the other just to take in the length of the place. Not easy with a sore neck. And she wasn't even counting the garages and guest house and cabana. If she turned far enough, she could see stables, too, a few hundred yards beyond. The gardens surrounding the house were equally opulent. Last night's rain and the humidity still hanging in the air made even the late autumn garden smell alive and lush.

"It might be big and fancy and new," Marie said, "but it doesn't have the beauty of Drake House. Nor the class."

A smile flickered over his lips.

A corresponding flutter seized her chest, despite her efforts to clamp it down.

"What?"

She shook her head. "Nothing, really. I just…I think that's the first time I've seen you smile since I came back."

The smile faded.

She wished she hadn't pointed it out. But it was probably better this way. His smile only reminded her of better times. Times she couldn't afford to think about now. She focused on the sprawling house. "Maybe you're right. Maybe Cliff has all the money he needs."

"I was thinking about that. Maybe it's not about money. Maybe it's about the one thing I've got that he doesn't. Drake House."

Chills trickled down Marie's spine. Could that be it? It seemed to make sense. "If you and Charlotte had children, Drake House would pass to them. But if you died without heirs, Cliff would finally get what he feels should have been his inheritance all along."

Brandon nodded. "It's hard for me to believe Cliff would take things that far, but I suppose it's possible. He and my father defined the term *sibling rivalry*. Maybe it's more about that than anything else."

Unfortunately Cliff wasn't home. After a brief exchange with the servant who answered the door, they followed his instructions and circled to the boathouse and long pier that reached into Chesapeake Bay. A lethal-looking speedboat bobbed in the water. A lethal-looking redhead lounged inside the craft.

"Brandon!" Isabella shouted from the yacht's deck. She flipped her hair over one shoulder and sat up in the boat, giving her employer the benefit of her full attention and her electric blue eyes. She artfully ignored Marie. "What a wonderful surprise. Are you coming out with us?"

Marie did her best to ignore the twinge of jealousy. Even in jeans and a leather bomber jacket, Isabella had the pin-up potential of a swimsuit model.

"*We* are here to have a word with Cliff."

"You can chat with Cliff on the boat. Really, Brandon, it's not an imposition to have one more. Cliff won't mind, I'm sure. I feel like I haven't seen you very much in the past few days." She leaned forward in her seat. Her unzipped jacket parted to reveal a low-cut top framing ample cleavage.

Marie tried her best not to let Isabella get to her. It was obvious she had the hots for Brandon. And likely his uncle Cliff, or she wouldn't be here on her day off. But whatever games she was playing with the Drake men, it wasn't any of Marie's business. She had to remember that.

Cliff emerged from the redbrick boathouse, a miniature mansion in itself. Dressed in a Burberry windbreaker, a cashmere sweater and perfectly tailored slacks, he looked every inch the wealthy playboy he was. His thick hair had gained some gray since the last time Marie saw him, but the new look only served to add sophistication to his list of charms.

He nodded to his nephew. "Brandon." Judging from his tone of voice, he wasn't as excited to see his nephew as Isabella was. He eyed Marie. "And…Marie Leonard, right?"

Marie nodded. Cliff had always intimidated her growing up. He'd seemed so confident, carefree and in control of his life. A man who lived big and wasn't ashamed to let the world envy him for it. He was the opposite of everything her humble, decorous father had instilled in her, and more than once she'd been totally bowled over by his presence. She could only hope now that she was an adult, she'd be able to handle him better. "Hello, Mr. Drake."

"Call me Cliff, please." He managed to look her up and down in a manner that was more flattering than intrusive. "You've grown up since the last time I saw you."

Marie held his gaze. She wasn't sure if Cliff's once-over was meant to bother Brandon or Isabella or both. But whatever was going on, she wanted no part of it. "I have a few things I'd like to ask you."

He raised his brows. "Sure. I'm glad you stopped by. I heard you were visiting Drake House."

"Visiting? My father died."

"Yes. A great loss. I'm so sorry."

Surprisingly, his tone sounded sincere. Maybe there was more to Clifford Drake than she'd ever guessed. Or maybe he was just trying to throw her off balance. "Thank you."

"You should come out on the boat. Racing over the water at high speed tends to take your mind off your problems. And it promises to be a lot more fun than hanging around old Brandon."

"We came to ask you some questions," Brandon said.

"Questions?" Cliff kept his gaze glued to Marie. "About what?"

"The recent deaths at Drake House. My father and Charlotte."

Cliff finally glanced at Brandon, as if gauging his nephew's reaction to his dead wife's name.

Brandon didn't move a muscle. Wavelets lapped against the pier's pilings.

Cliff looked back to Marie. "Tragedies, to be sure. What makes you think I can tell you anything?"

"You're part of the family. You live nearby."

"I do live nearby, but if you hadn't figured this out yet, the Drake family isn't exactly close."

Marie looked past Cliff to where Isabella was climbing out of the speedboat and onto the pier. Apparently she'd grown tired of being out of the spotlight and intended to take it back.

Marie gave Cliff a businesslike smile. "I know you have plans, so I'll make this short."

A lazy grin spread over Cliff's lips. He glanced in Brandon's direction and lowered one lid in a wink. "What can I say? I'm in demand."

"What are you men talking about?" Walking up behind Brandon, Isabella slipped her hands onto his shoulders and started kneading his muscles.

Brandon stiffened.

Cliff's easy smile faded. He shot Isabella a warning stare.

Isabella withdrew her hands and wormed her way into the circle, Brandon and Cliff on either side.

Marie shook her head. Let Isabella play her games. Marie had more important things to focus on. "Mr.

Drake? Did you see either Charlotte or my father around the time of their deaths?"

"I told you, it's Cliff. And yes, I saw your father a day or two before he died."

Of the two, Marie would have guessed it more likely for Cliff to have seen Charlotte. Or at least to have noticed her. But six months was a long time. Maybe he didn't remember, provided he didn't have anything to do with killing her. "Where was my father when you saw him?"

"Near the harbor. You know that bed-and-breakfast called The Seven Gables or some such?"

"Sophie Caldwell's place? Was he with her?"

"No. He was talking to that pain-in-the-ass developer. Perry. And let me tell you, your father didn't look too happy."

Marie could imagine. Shelley had said Ned Perry was trying to buy waterfront, including Drake House, and build condos. No idea would insult her father's sensibilities more. "What about Charlotte? Did you see her before her death?"

"No."

Marie and Brandon exchanged looks. He seemed to be as uneasy with Cliff's answer as she was. The abrupt answer felt a little too quick, a little too pat. "You're sure?"

"Absolutely."

Brandon eyed his uncle. "Charlotte died six months ago. That's a long time."

"You want an alibi?" Cliff chuckled, the sound more taunt than real laugh. "I was sailing. A regatta in the U.K. Stop by the yacht club. I'll take you on the yacht that won and show you the trophy."

Marie's stomach sank. Beyond Cliff, she didn't have much of a list of people who could benefit from Charlotte's death. She had no leads. All she had were the words of a ghost. Words Brandon didn't even believe.

Cliff narrowed his eyes on his nephew. "So why are you playing like this is some sort of murder investigation? I know about the vodka bottle. You might have been able to keep that part out of the papers, but I have my sources." He shot Isabella a little smile.

The maid tilted her chin up and gave Cliff a frown. She laid a hand on Brandon's arm. "I'm sorry, Brandon. I didn't mean to say anything. Really I didn't. I was just so upset that she would do that to you. She didn't deserve what she had. Drake House. You. She didn't deserve any of it." Flirty lilt gone, Isabella's voice rang with a hard edge.

Brandon's lips flattened. "Isabella, stop."

"It's true. I was hoping you'd see it after she died." The maid tilted her head in Marie's direction. "And if you think this one deserves you, you're going to be disappointed all over again."

BRANDON HAD NEVER BEEN as glad to leave a place as he was walking back to the car from Cliff's boathouse. Every moment of that encounter had been awkward and painful and teeth-grindingly frustrating.

"Did you hear the venom in her voice?" Marie asked.

"Isabella has a few issues." To put it mildly.

"Issues like she wants to be the lady of Drake House."

"Or The Manor at Drake Acres. I don't think it matters much to her." He let out a pent-up breath. "I think we're going to need to keep an eye on her."

"Do you think she might have killed Charlotte?"

"I don't see it. She couldn't have gotten Charlotte into the car and crashed it by herself." He still wasn't sure how anyone could have done that except for Charlotte herself. But since he wasn't about to get into a debate with Marie about the existence of ghosts, he'd let that part slide for now. "Isabella could have gotten someone to help her. She's good at convincing men to do things for her."

"Men? Like who? Cliff was racing one of his yachts."

"There are men besides Cliff." They rounded the far corner of the house and started toward the circle in front of the house's grand entrance where his car waited. Josef spotted them and climbed out of the car. Brandon kept his voice low. "Take Josef. He lost his fiancée about a year ago. He's got to be lonely. And he knows his way around cars."

"You think Josef—"

"Or Phil Cardon."

Marie frowned, as if searching her memory for the name. "The guy who works at Thornton Garden Center?"

Brandon nodded. "He has done some work at Drake House from time to time. And he worked on the gardens with Lexie. He was pretty interested in Isabella."

"I can imagine. But was he interested enough to help her commit murder?"

Brandon shrugged.

"How about the guy from Drake Enterprises? The one who came to Drake House?"

"Doug Heller? I could see it." Truthfully, he couldn't see it at all. Any of it. He still couldn't wrap his mind around the idea that Charlotte was murdered. That someone he knew was responsible. Maybe he was just in denial, but this whole conversation with Marie didn't seem real to him. More like a guessing game played purely for amusement. He was much more concerned with finding who had tried to kill Marie. "Do you think Isabella could have been the one who tried to throw you off the roof last night?"

Marie's steps slowed. "Maybe. She's taller than I am. And strong. I don't know."

"Maybe that's what we should focus on."

"I told you, I think it's all related."

He nodded. He was waiting for her to say that. "Think and know are two different things. And until we know it's related and know who wants you dead, we need to keep our options open. I don't want to overlook anyone."

They walked for a moment without speaking, the click of their shoes on the brick path the only sound. The sun beamed down from a sky that seemed shockingly blue after the dreariness of the day before. Too bad their situation wasn't as clear and pleasant as the weather.

"So what do we do?"

He wanted to suggest buying her a plane ticket, sending her back to Michigan where she'd be safe…and away from him. But he knew what her reaction would be. "Set some traps and see what happens."

As they approached the car, Josef opened the back door. Marie climbed inside. The chauffeur circled the car and opened the opposite door for Brandon. When it came to his job, Josef was precise and efficient. Could he be as precise and efficient when it came to killing someone? Especially if a young redhead, beautiful beyond his dreams, seduced him into it?

Brandon lowered himself into the car and waited for Josef to take his place behind the wheel. "Josef?"

"Yes, sir?" His accent was thick and warm and tinged with respect. Just the right tone.

"Take us back to Drake House. Then you can have the rest of the day off. And the night. We'll see you again tomorrow morning."

"Sir? May I ask why?"

"I've been asking a lot of you the past few days." He paused for dramatic effect...he hoped. "And we've learned something very disturbing about Isabella Faust. I'd like to handle it myself. If we need to go anywhere, we'll use Ms. Leonard's rental car."

Josef nodded and pulled away, leaving The Manor at Drake Acres behind. "Very good, sir."

SITTING IN A CRAMPED RENTAL CAR with a leg injury was not a good idea. Too bad Brandon hadn't realized that before he and Marie had jumped in her car in a damn fool attempt to follow Isabella's little yellow sports car when she'd returned from her day with Cliff. The trap he'd set for Josef turned out to be nothing. Nothing at all. The chauffeur had made no move to warn Isabella of their suspicions. He hadn't gone anywhere, and a call to the phone company had proved he hadn't made any phone calls.

Brandon shifted his leg into a more comfortable position. "I feel like an idiot spying on my employees. Especially since they don't seem to be doing a damn thing out of the ordinary."

Eyes on the road and the yellow car in front of them, Marie let out a sigh. The lights from the dash cast her face in a green glow, a color that would make anyone look like death warmed over. But not Marie. She looked as vibrant and determined as ever.

God help him.

"What is it?" he asked her.

"Nothing, really. I'm relieved Josef isn't tangled up with Isabella, but his life seems kind of sad."

"How so?"

"I don't know. Just what Shelley told me. Moving to a country where he doesn't know anyone. Losing his fiancée. He seems so alone."

Brandon nodded. Widowed. Alone. As Brandon himself had been before Marie had returned. As he would be again after she left.

He shook his head. If only he could forget all that, accept it. But it was impossible with her sitting only inches away. The scent of her, warm and spicy, wrapped around him, and he longed to feel the softness of her skin again.

Riding around with Marie in this cramped little car wasn't one of his best ideas.

He gripped his cane in both hands and remembered the bruising hidden under the high collar of her coat. He couldn't have Marie. He couldn't even let himself want her. But he could protect her. He could keep her safe.

"I finally got a hold of Lexie." Marie kept her focus on the road. "She said her records show Phil Cardon was working with her on a garden in Easton when Charlotte died. She said they were on the job site until sunset every night. There's no way he could have driven all the way to Drake House before the time of Charlotte's accident."

Another name off the list. "Doug is stopping by Drake House for a chat tomorrow. But I can't imagine he has anything to do with this."

Marie piloted the car down Main Street and into the heart of town. Shops and cafés lined the street, festooned with wreaths and lights and tinsel.

Christmas.

An ache settled into Brandon's gut. From the time he could remember, Christmas had been centered on the ball and charity auction. He remembered his mother presiding over the decoration. Then Edwin and, to a lesser extent, Charlotte. When he'd lost all of them, there had seemed no point to go on. He hadn't even felt bad about letting the tradition die. Or maybe he'd felt so bad about everything else that he hadn't noticed.

But now?

The time Marie had been here had been filled with turmoil and pain. Still, by comparison, he felt more alive than he had in years. And for the first time, the thought of Jenkins Cove going through a Christmas season without the charity ball felt…not right.

As the yellow car reached the outskirts of town, it slowed and turned into a lot. Brandon glanced at Marie. "Did you see that?"

"Yes." Marie drove to a spot near the street where Isabella turned, and pulled to the curb. Beyond a small parking lot sat a little restaurant and bar known to the locals as the spot for soft-shell crab in season and cheap booze all year-round. The Duck Blind.

"Does Rufus Shea still own this place?"

"I think so." Brandon frowned. Even though Rufus Shea had cleaned up his act and his tavern in recent years, the former town drunk wasn't the type of man Brandon could picture Marie having anything to do with. "How do you know Rufus Shea?"

"I knew his son."

Brandon nodded. He'd known Rufus's son, Simon, too, though not well. The kid had been younger. The quintessential troublemaker from the wrong side of the tracks. Brandon had been at Harvard when he'd heard about the kid's death. A lifetime ago. "I wonder what brings Isabella here?" He nodded out the window as the auburn-haired beauty pulled the door open and slipped inside.

"Should we find out?" Marie took the key from the ignition and got out of the car.

Brandon followed. They entered in time to catch Isabella stride past the counter and bar stools and turn into the restaurant. They followed. Sturdy round tables covered with red and green tablecloths dotted the modest-sized room. A good crowd of people filled the place, dining on plates of crab cakes and passing bowls of stewed tomatoes and lima beans served family style. The din of conversation bounced off paneled walls, and the sweet and tangy scent of seafood hung in the air.

Isabella made a beeline for a table in the far corner. She slipped into a chair beside a man.

A man Brandon recognized immediately.

He grabbed Marie's arm, stopping her before she was spotted. He leaned close and spoke into her ear. "Ned Perry. She's meeting with Ned Perry."

Marie looked toward the table, eyes wide. "The real estate developer? Do you think this might have something to do with Drake House?"

"I don't know. But I aim to find out."

MARIE SNUGGLED her coat tight around her shoulders against the cool morning. Kneeling down beside

Brandon's town car, she examined the tire. The white chalk line was still there, untouched.

She'd gotten the idea from her parking hassles in college. It was a trick the parking authority used. Mark the tire with chalk. If the chalk is still there, the car hasn't moved. In this case, that meant Josef hadn't moved. Not the entire night.

At least they could cross him off the list. Cliff as well. And probably Phil Cardon. But Isabella seemed to be neck deep in whatever was going on. And Marie was betting Ned Perry was helping her.

Marie wound through the east garden and back to the kitchen. Frost sparkled on the concrete bench, the fountain and the white shells that covered the path. Not quite like snow at Christmastime, but the extra sparkle lent Drake House a little magic of the season. Magic that was sorely lacking.

She found Brandon in the kitchen, sitting at the stone counter where she'd eaten cookies as a child. He sipped a cup of coffee and watched Shelley sauté vegetables for one of her extravagant breakfasts. Mouthwatering aromas and thick steam wafted from the pan. Brandon looked up at Marie and arched his brows in silent question.

She shook her head.

He leaned back in his chair, relieved.

One more name off the suspect list. Marie took a cup of coffee and tried to concentrate on drinking it without burning her lips and tongue.

A knock sounded on the kitchen door.

Marie jumped at the sound. She glanced through the mullioned glass. A pair of watery blue eyes stared straight at her.

Shelley wiped her hands and scampered to open the door.

The operations manager of Drake Enterprises stepped inside. "Brandon?"

Brandon nodded and stood, leaning heavily on his cane. "Thanks for coming, Doug. We'll talk in the office." Giving Marie a glance, he led Doug Heller from the kitchen. Brandon had told her he planned to pump the manager for information about Perry. And, of course, he wanted to ask a few questions of Heller himself.

As soon as they disappeared into the household office and closed the door behind them, Shelley made a tsking noise under her breath.

Marie focused on the housekeeper. "What is it, Shelley?"

"I can just imagine. Probably Ned Perry again."

Marie nodded vaguely, not wanting to let on that Shelley's guess was right on the nose. "Does this Mr. Perry stop by often?"

"No. He hasn't for a while. He doesn't have the nerve. But then he doesn't have to when he has someone already in the house lobbying for him."

"Someone in the house? Who?"

"Isabella."

Marie's pulse launched into double time. She didn't know why she hadn't thought of asking Shelley about this sooner. The woman seemed to know everyone's business. And she had no qualms about spreading the news around. "Why would Isabella lobby for Ned Perry?"

"They have a deal."

"A deal?" This was getting better all the time.

"She says she's buying one of the condos down by

the yacht club. But I think she wants a piece of Drake House. She's always wanted Drake House, you know. Although I don't know how she thinks Ned Perry is going to get his hands on it."

It hadn't occurred to Marie that Isabella wanted Drake House, not until her performance yesterday. What other secrets could Shelley tell her? "Why do you think Isabella wants Drake House?"

"Just ask her." Shelley pulled a knife from the block and started dicing shallots with more gusto than called for. The knife made a sharp snap each time it hit the cutting board. "When she first came to work here, she told me that one day she'd be lady of the house. 'It's only a matter of time,' she'd say. Hogwash. Mr. Brandon saw nothing in her. He only saw his Charlotte."

Shelley shook her head. Scooping up the shallots with the flat of her blade, she feathered them into the sauté pan and turned up the heat. An onionlike tang flavored the air. "After Charlotte died, Isabella got more aggressive. I told her it was no use. And it wasn't. Mr. Brandon is heartbroken. He lives only for his foundation and this house. He'll never marry again. Charlotte was the only woman he could ever love. She was perfect. You'd do well to remember that, too."

"Me?" If Marie hadn't been sitting, she would have stepped back under the assault. "What does this have to do with me?"

"I've seen you with him. Trying to make him smile. Trying to make him do things for you. You'd be better off leaving him alone." Shelley gathered a handful of dirty utensils and carried them to one of the huge sinks. She pushed up the sleeves of her blouse, revealing muscled arms. "I'm not trying to be mean. I'm telling you for your own good. He belongs to Charlotte. No other woman is wanted around here."

Marie stared at Shelley, not sure she heard the woman right. Hadn't she joked to herself about Shelley's resemblance to the fictional Mrs. Danvers? And now this on the heels of Isabella's comments yesterday? "Anything between Brandon and me is in the past, Shelley. It's over. You don't have to feel threatened by me."

"I'm just telling you the way things are. You seem like a nice girl, and I always respected your father. I wouldn't like to see you get hurt."

Marie nodded, not sure if Shelley's words held more motherly concern or threat.

Shelley thrust the utensils under running water. The scent of dishwashing soap mixed with the aroma from the stove. "While we're on the subject, I've talked to a handyman who occasionally does work around here. Phil Cardon. He has some hours free later today, so I hired him to help you pack up your father's things."

So Shelley was shoving her out of the house. Protecting Brandon's honor and Charlotte's memory, no doubt. Unless she had a more personal agenda. "I have time. I'm on personal leave from my job. There's no hurry."

"Well, you aren't the only one this affects, Marie. We have to think about Brandon. He likes his privacy. Having a guest in the house is tough on him."

Marie pushed herself back from the counter and picked up her coffee. She was getting a little tired of being in Shelley's crosshairs this morning. And while Marie knew her presence wasn't any easier on Brandon than it was on her, she wasn't going to let the housekeeper chase her out before she got her answers. "Maybe we should ask Brandon."

"There are other concerns, too." Shelley smiled, backpedaling.

Marie should just walk out of the room, leave Shelley stewing. Unfortunately she was never one to leave a leading comment hanging in the air without asking the question that went with it. "Such as?"

"It's very difficult to run the house when I'm not living here."

Now it was becoming clear. "You want to move into my father's quarters."

"Those rooms are for the person who is running Drake House. They aren't your father's personal property."

Marie couldn't argue with that, even though her father had lived in those rooms for forty years. "As soon as I finish tying up some loose ends, you can have your rooms."

Shelley nodded her graying head. "Good. I'm glad we understand each other."

Marie gave Shelley a broad smile. "Yes. We understand each other. But I don't need your handyman's help. No one is to touch my father's things but me."

Shelley didn't answer.

Marie clenched the hot mug. The moment she left the house, Shelley would probably have an army of handymen erasing her father's presence from Drake House. She'd have to ask Brandon to make sure that didn't happen.

"Perhaps you'd do a favor for me now."

The woman was asking for a favor? After everything she'd thrown at Marie in the past few minutes?

"I need you to move your car to the parking area

next to the carriage house. I have a decorator coming in to take measurements, and your vehicle will be in the way."

Marie had the sneaking suspicion Shelley thought everything about her was in the way. But as much as Shelley's grasping annoyed her, she had to admit life went on. An old and important mansion like Drake House needed a full-time caretaker, and Brandon had given the job to Shelley. With the job came the living quarters. She couldn't deny Shelley that.

But that didn't mean she'd let the woman push her out before she'd exhausted every lead. Finding her father's killer, and Charlotte's as well, came first. "Measure all you want, Shelley, but don't touch my father's things. Do you understand me?"

Shelley pursed her lips and raised her chin. "As long as you clear out the rooms in a timely manner. Now will you move your vehicle? My decorator will be here any minute." She glanced at a clock on the wall for emphasis.

Marie plunked her mug on the countertop, grabbed her keys and coat and gladly left the kitchen to Shelley Zachary.

Out in the cool morning, her car started on the third try. She'd have to take it in to the rental agency. Have them replace the battery or give her a new car.

She piloted the rental around the kitchen entrance's circle drive and joined with the drive leading to the carriage house, curving along the edge of the water.

Steely waves echoed the color of the sky and pounded rocks edging the shoreline. She approached the turn to the carriage house. Although the land around Drake House was fairly flat, this part of the drive dipped slightly, making her car accelerate. She pressed her foot to the brake pedal. It gripped, then softened.

Then plunged to the floorboards.

Marie tried the brakes again. Again they pushed to the floor. She didn't have time to think. Didn't even have time to panic. Blood rushing in her ears, she gripped the wheel and steered. The car canted to the side. Tires skidded on loose gravel.

The car jolted over rock and plunged into water.

Chapter Eleven

Marie hung forward in her seat belt. The air bag softened in front of her like a limp balloon, only dregs of air left. Her ears rang. Her already sore head and neck ached. Her feet felt so very cold.

Pushing down the air bag, she fought to clear her mind. Water sloshed over the car's hood. It covered the pedals and crept up the floor mat, swamping her feet to the ankles.

What a mess.

She looked out the driver's window. The car balanced on the gray rock that lined the shoreline, preventing erosion. Even though the nose tilted down into the water, the back end of the car was still high, if not totally dry.

She was lucky. If she had been going faster, she'd be out in the bay right now. As it was, she might have to do a little swimming, or at least wading, but she still had time to get out.

Trying to steady her trembling fingers, she found the buckle of her seat belt and released it. She groped the armrest, locating the controls for the power windows. She pressed the button to lower the driver's side.

Nothing happened.

She tried again. Damn. The water or the impact must have shorted out the car's battery or jostled the wires free. Not that it hadn't been half drained before she'd even gotten behind the wheel.

There was no reason to panic. Although the water seemed to creep higher by the second, she still had time to escape. But she needed to move.

She grasped the lock and pulled it up, releasing it manually. Fitting her fingers into the handle, she pulled it and shoved her shoulder into the door at the same time.

The door didn't budge.

A sob caught in her throat. She tried again. Again, it wouldn't open. Water bore down on the door, sealing it from the outside.

What was she going to do?

She closed her eyes and focused on her breathing. In and out. In and out. She couldn't let herself panic. There had to be a way out. She just had to stay calm enough to think, stay calm enough to find it.

If water pressure from the outside was forcing the door closed, then equaling the pressure would free the door. She just had to wait for the car to sink. The slight odor of fish clogged her throat. The relentless lap of waves drummed in beat with her pulse.

She'd never been afraid of water. Her father had insisted she take swimming lessons so she wouldn't suffer from the fear as he had. But the thought of letting the car sink, letting herself be trapped underwater…she didn't know if she could go through with it.

The car listed farther forward, the heavy engine dragging it down. The water rose to her knees. It crept over the seat.

A shudder came from the back of the vehicle. Marie twisted in her seat. Sore muscles in her neck protesting, she strained to see where the movement had come from.

Behind her, the shoreline seemed to move away.

The car jolted again. Oh God. She knew what was happening. The back wheels were thunking down the rocks along the shoreline. Without brakes to stop them, they would keep rolling, pushing the car farther into the bay.

Where the water was deep.

A sound came from her throat, an involuntary whimper.

She pulled the emergency brake. The lever moved easily. Too easily. It wasn't working, either.

She tried to breathe, struggling to remember the way Sophie had showed her. All she could think about was the car's nose diving deep. The car flipping over. Would she be able to get out if that happened? Would she even be conscious by the time it settled on the bottom?

She couldn't wait. She had to do something now.

She pulled her feet up out of the water. Twisting out from behind the steering wheel, she aimed the heels of her boots at the driver's window. Pulling her knees up to her chest, she gasped in a lungful of oxygen and kicked with all her strength.

Glass exploded into tiny pieces.

CURSING HIS LEG, Brandon raced for the edge of the water. He'd been walking Doug Heller to the door when he'd seen Marie's car go over the edge. For a second, he'd been stunned and confused. His body had burst into a run before his brain had caught up.

Marie was in the water. Maybe trapped in her car. Maybe hurt. He had to move. He had to reach her in time.

Pain clawed through his damaged tendons with each stride. He gripped his cane, stabbing it into the ground, pushing his legs faster.

He wouldn't lose Marie.

He reached the crest of the shoreline. Water stretched in front of him, waves lapping on rock. A light mass showed through the undulating waves. The car. It was submerged.

He stumbled on the rock, almost going down to his knees. She couldn't—

"Brandon."

He turned to the sound of her voice.

She huddled on the sharp rock, ten yards down the shoreline. Her clothing was soaked, her hair dark with water. She struggled to stand.

He scrambled over rock. His cane slipped from his hand and clattered into a crevice. He didn't care. He kept going. The only important thing was reaching Marie. The only important thing was that she was safe.

He wrapped her in his arms.

She clung to him, wet and cold and shaking. She looked up at him, her breath warm on his face.

He brought his mouth down on hers. Needy. Devouring the very life force of her. She tasted just the way he remembered. Warm and strong and oh so alive. He moved his lips over her face, her neck. Taking in all of her. Soaking in the feel of her body, the beat of her heart against his. He felt he'd waited forever for this. Wanted it. Dreamed about it. Pushed the dreams away. But he didn't deny himself now. He couldn't. It didn't matter that it was all wrong. That they'd get hurt in the end. That it could go nowhere. He'd almost lost her, but she was here. She'd almost died, but now she lived.

And God help him, whatever happened next, he didn't know how he'd ever let her go.

MARIE PULLED her big wool sweater tight around her shoulders and shifted closer to the fire. Her neck had changed from painful to stiff and painful. And although she was now dry, the chill hadn't left her bones. It felt as if it never would.

"Here." Brandon pushed a fresh cup of hot tea into her hands.

"Thanks." She wrapped her fingers around the cup's heat. He'd been hovering over her since he'd found her on the rocks, having escaped from the car and swum to shore. And even though she hated to admit it, she loved him taking care of her. It had been a long time since someone took care of her. Since she'd last lived at Drake House with a father who took care of everybody.

But Brandon wasn't anything like her father.

She could still feel the desperate press of his body against hers. She could still taste his kiss. It had been everything she wanted, the passion between them unleashed, the barriers broken. But even though he looked at her now with the same fire in his eyes, she knew their moment had changed nothing.

And that was what confused her the most.

Brandon lowered himself into a nearby chair.

How she wished he'd sit closer. How she wanted him to wrap his arm around her and kiss her again. She knew he'd do it if she asked. After that kiss she was even pretty sure he still loved her. Not that he'd admit it. Not that it mattered.

Brandon blamed himself for loving her. He blamed his feelings for causing his wife's death. And unless she proved to him Charlotte hadn't taken her own life, there was no way he'd forgive himself. Not enough to find happiness. At least not happiness with Marie.

And there was no way she wanted to suffer that kind of heartbreak again. She knew better this time.

Brandon checked his watch. "Hammer should be here any minute."

Marie almost groaned. "I'm not looking forward to explaining this to Hammer. He already thinks I'm making things up. My father's murder. The break-in. Even the roof. He's going to think I drove into the water myself. He's going to be more convinced than ever that I'm a crackpot."

Brandon didn't disagree. Instead he leaned forward and looked her in the eye. "Don't mention your father's murder. Or Charlotte's."

She wanted to protest that it was all related, but she'd told him that too many times before. "I won't. He'll have me committed for sure."

"Just focus on the attempts to hurt you. That's all we can do. It's all Hammer can help with, anyway."

And it was all Brandon believed.

A heavy feeling settled into the pit of Marie's stomach. This whole thing was a no-win situation. Finding evidence that didn't exist. Falling in love with Brandon all over again when she could only hope for more of the same pain.

Brandon shifted in his chair. "Where were you going this morning? The last I saw, you were having coffee."

He looked up at her again, this time his expression less insistent and more filled with worry.

"I wasn't going anywhere. Shelley asked me to move my car."

"Why?"

She explained about the decorator and Shelley's pressure to clean out her father's things. She wanted to tell him the rest, too. The way Shelley worshiped Charlotte. The way she'd warned Marie to stay away. But it all seemed too close after the kiss. Shelley was more perceptive than Marie had given her credit for.

Brandon groaned. "I should have been more on top of that. You'll have as much time as you need."

"Thanks."

He kept his eyes on her face. His brows dipped low. "What else?"

"I'm going back to the psychomanteum." She hadn't known that was her plan until she said it. But once the words were out, she knew it was what she needed to do.

"Are you sure?"

The thought made her nervous. But not more nervous than the idea of never finding out who killed her father and Charlotte. Not more nervous than waiting for the police to track down whoever was trying to kill her, especially when Chief Hammer seemed determined to chalk it up to her paranoid imagination. And it didn't make her more nervous than the growing feelings she had for Brandon and the certainty that she was heading for the same anguish she'd suffered ten years before. "I'm sure."

It seemed to take a lot of effort for Brandon to nod this

time. "Then I'll take you. I'm not letting you out of my sight until you're safely on a plane back to Michigan."

The cold settled deeper into her bones.

"Mr. Brandon?" Shelley called from the doorway. "Chief Hammer and Officer Draper are here."

Marie took a deep breath and braced herself for another round with the Jenkins Cove police.

MARIE STARED at the flickering candlelight reflected in the mirror. She tried to clear her mind, to relax, but a jitter circulated through her bloodstream like too much espresso, and she didn't seem to be able to focus on anything. After more than an hour, she'd given up trying to reach her father. Now she'd switched her focus to Charlotte. If this didn't work, she was out of options.

She breathed deeply, as Sophie had instructed. In and out. In and out. But all she smelled was the dusty odor of an old house. All she felt was a light head.

"Charlotte? Where are you?"

No scent. No voice.

"Charlotte? Please. I need your help."

Again nothing.

Marie stared at the mirror. Her own face stared back. She didn't get it. If Charlotte had been trying to tell her she'd been murdered, if she'd wanted Marie to find proof and seek justice, why wasn't she answering? Why wasn't she helping now?

"I can't find anything to prove your murder. I don't know where to look." She buried her head in her hands. If Charlotte couldn't communicate anymore, all this was no use. She might as well go back to Michigan. At least that way, she'd get far away from Brandon. She'd save herself the heartbreak of loving a man who wouldn't let himself love her back.

Tears stung the back of her eyes. She drew in a shuddering breath.

Jasmine.

Marie raised her head. Swiping at her eyes, she stared at the mirror. She felt something. A pressure. A presence. Candlelight flickered from behind her. Her vision became unfocused. "Charlotte? Tell me who killed you. Give me some kind of sign."

The scent of jasmine faded. Another odor took over the room. Something harsh. Sharp fumes stung her eyes.

Gasoline.

The whoosh of flame stole the air from her lungs. Heat seared her skin. Pain. Burning.

A scream ripped from Marie's throat. She shielded her face with her hands. She wasn't on fire. It wasn't real. She knew it…and yet the brightness flooded her vision, the roar of flame deafened her, the heat made her feel as if she were dying. "Charlotte, please. Who did this? Who did this to you?"

Footsteps thunked up the stairs.

She dragged her hands from her face and stared into the mirror.

The image was faint, like a cloud on her vision from the pressure of fingertips against closed lids. Petals. A stem. A single leaf.

A childlike etching of a simple flower took shape. A flower with cupped petals. A tulip.

The door flew open behind her. Brandon's reflection filled the mirror. Broad shoulders, dark brows, worried eyes. "Marie! For God's sake, what happened?"

Marie stared deeply into the silvered glass, but the

image had faded and was gone. All she could see was candlelight and shadows playing over Brandon's face.

Sophie joined him in the doorway. "Sweetheart? Are you okay?"

She felt weak. Sick. And although the burning sensation had stopped, she felt numb as if she were now covered with thick scars. "No, I'm not. I'm not okay at all."

Chapter Twelve

"I know you don't believe me."

Brandon's throat pinched. He followed her up the stairs that led to the upper floors of the east wing. Swallowing what she'd experienced in the psychomanteum was definitely a challenge. He'd never been one to believe in things he couldn't see with his own eyes, hear with his own ears, touch with his own hand. "I've never had experiences like that, Marie. I'm trying to understand."

She stopped on the landing and spun to face him. "Go to the psychomanteum. Obviously Charlotte is trying to contact you. She's just using me to do it."

"I don't need to sit in Sophie Caldwell's room, Marie. I know what Charlotte went through. I was there."

Even in the dim light he could see her gaze flit over the right side of his face.

He clutched the head of his cane. He hated the thought that Marie could see his scars and imperfections every time she looked at his face or witnessed his limp. He wished he could be the same man for her that he'd been that summer ten years ago. Despite the raw emotion still between them, he knew damn well it was too late for that.

Just as it was too late for Charlotte.

"What are you looking for up here?"

Marie resumed climbing the stairs. "The other night I smelled Charlotte's scent near the window in her study. I looked around, but couldn't find anything."

"I had Edwin give Charlotte's personal things to her family and the rest to charity. He wanted to auction off the furniture at the Christmas Ball."

"Shelley said you canceled the ball."

"Edwin and Charlotte put on the ball. It just didn't seem right to do it without them. And to tell you the truth, I didn't feel up to having people in the house."

"My father loved the ball. He loved Christmas."

"Which is why I can't see having it without him."

Reaching the top of the stairs, she paused once again to face him. "I think he would like it to go on. I think it would be a fitting tribute, to both my father and Charlotte. Besides, the Drake Foundation does wonderful things with the auction money, things that help a lot of people."

Leave it to Marie to see past the pain, to focus on the people in need and a tribute to the memories of those gone. "You are a strong woman, Marie." He wanted to touch her, to run his fingers through her hair, to kiss her the way he had by the water. He wished he could kiss her like that every day for the rest of his life. He gripped his cane in both fists.

"Thanks. I don't feel very strong."

"Well, you are. That's probably why Charlotte has contacted you instead of me. She knows you can handle it. She knows you're a fighter."

"You're a fighter, too." Her wide, caramel eyes looked straight into his, as though she believed what she was saying, as though she meant every word.

"I like the man I am in your eyes. I always have."

"You are that man, Brandon."

How he wished he could believe that. How he wished all the mistakes he'd made in his life would disappear and he could be as pure and strong and righteous as he'd felt when he'd fallen in love with Marie all those years ago.

But even then he'd already given Charlotte his mother's ring. Even then he hadn't lived up to Marie's image of him. "I'm not. I don't know if I ever was. But when you look at me, I can pretend. And that will have to be enough."

She reached out and took his hand.

He clasped her fingers. Her skin felt impossibly soft, her bones fragile. But it was all an illusion. Marie was strong and tough and unflinching in her caring for others and in her belief that good would win in the end. She was everything he was not. Everything he'd lost over the years. Everything he'd never had. It was impossible to go back, impossible to change things. But at least for the moment, he could hold her hand and pretend. "Lead on."

"DO YOU SMELL IT?" Marie leaned close to the desk where she'd smelled the jasmine before she'd been dragged to the roof. The scent tickled her nose, light and sweet. Barely there, yet every bit grounded in reality.

Brandon tilted his head and gave the air a sniff. "Where?"

It grew stronger. She gestured for him to move closer. "Right here. All around."

He stepped beside her. Almost close enough for her to feel his body heat. Almost close enough that if she shifted to the side, their arms would touch.

Breathing slowly, he finally shook his head. "Where does it seem to be coming from?"

She leaned toward the window. Sure enough, it was stronger here. "Not the desk. Maybe the window."

He followed, breathing deep, a frown still lining his brow.

Marie stood still. Cold flowed over her, digging deep and sucking the warmth from her skin. She glanced back at Brandon. "Do you feel that?"

"The draft?"

"A few days ago I would have thought it was a draft, too." She raised her palm to the window. The air felt still. "This is not coming from outside. But the scent is strongest here." She gestured to the mullioned window.

"I...I can smell it." Brandon's voice rang low and steady, not questioning anymore, but sure.

Goosebumps peppered Marie's skin. "Do you feel her?"

"I...maybe. No. I don't know."

Marie peered through the rippled glass. The faint light of a slivered moon reflected off the waves of Chesapeake Bay. Below the window, the east garden nestled, ready for winter.

The garden where she'd first felt the still cold that was surrounding them now. "The garden."

"Edwin had that garden redesigned this fall."

Yes. She remembered that. But she hadn't put it all together. A trill reverberated along her nerves. "Maybe that's it. Let's go down to the garden." It didn't take them long to retrace their steps down the staircase. They wound through the dimly lit house to the kitchen and headed for the exit.

"Mr. Brandon?"

Marie jumped at the woman's voice.

Brandon spun around. "Shelley? Isn't it kind of late? What are you doing here?"

Shelley smiled sweetly at her boss. "Just taking care of some loose ends. Can I get you something?" She glanced at Marie, at their joined hands. The smile faded.

"No. We're fine. It's late." Brandon gave Marie's hand a little squeeze, then slipped his fingers free.

A weight shifted into Marie's chest.

"It's a big house. A lot to do," Shelley rattled on. "I can see why Edwin lived in the house. It's the only way to get everything done. And he didn't have anything to do with the cooking."

Marie knew Brandon wasn't going to offer the butler quarters, not until she was done with them. But she half expected him to let Shelley move into one of the guest rooms. And she had to admit, having someone else living in the house would make it easier for him to keep his distance, easier for them both.

"You're right, Shelley," Brandon said. "You are trying to do way too much. We'll have to start interviewing for cooks. Let me know when you have some good prospects lined up."

"Cooks?"

"Unless you'd rather take applicants for the butler's job."

"I'll get some cooks lined up right away, sir." She glanced at Marie, and gave her a somewhat apologetic smile.

"Good night." Brandon gave Shelley a nod. He held

the door open for Marie, and she slipped through into the night.

Oyster shells crunched under their feet. The night was cool, but even so, it felt balmy compared to the frigid air in Charlotte's study. Marie had heard cold spots were thought to be caused by spirits' attempt to manifest themselves. But she hadn't really connected those dots the first time she'd passed through the east garden. She wouldn't miss it again.

They wound their way to the garden. Holly and boxwood flanked the path. A plastic-covered fountain hulked near the house, its musical trickle silenced in preparation for the freezing temperatures of winter. The white concrete bench she'd spotted from the window glowed in the artful landscape lighting, nearly as bright as the shells at their feet.

"What are we looking for?"

"Search me." Brandon jabbed the fountain's covering with the tip of his cane. "This garden was redone after Charlotte's death. What was your father's favorite feature of this garden?"

Marie glanced at him. Did he now believe? She didn't know. Maybe he didn't, either. But at least he was trying. He was keeping his mind open. He was supporting her.

"My father. What did he like?" Marie blew a breath through tense lips. "I have no clue. My father was never into nature."

"Charlotte loved the rose garden on the west side of the house. And the gardens around the boathouse."

Marie shook her head. "I have a feeling it's this garden." The scent tickled Marie's senses, as if a confirmation of her belief. "Jasmine."

"Where?"

She turned around slowly. It seemed to be everywhere, faint in the outside air. Too faint. "I can't tell. I can hardly smell it."

"There must have been something about this garden that your father liked. He was the one who had it redesigned. I left it all up to him. I couldn't have cared less at the time."

What did her father like? "I don't know what it would be. I didn't know him to ever be passionate about gardens. Drake House, that's all he really cared about. He loved Drake House."

"That doesn't tell us anything."

"Wait. Maybe it does. I have an idea." She took the side path and wound her way through loosely mulched plants. She stopped at the concrete bench and sat down facing the house.

Landscape lighting shot upward, highlighting the house. The dark bushes stood out in sharp relief against the mansion's snow-white siding. Columns soared up to the third floor where the slate roof took over, all sharp angles and graceful slopes. In the summer, the fountain's magic would play against the backdrop of it all, its music adding to the mansion's grandeur.

Brandon sat down beside her.

Shivers prickled over her skin. "This is it. This is my father's favorite part of this garden."

He squinted at the bushes, the fountain, the smaller plants protected by mulch. "What is it?"

"My father loved Drake House more than anything, except maybe me. You have to admit, the house looks spectacular from this vantage point."

Brandon didn't look up. His eyes were still locked on the mulched plants at the bench's base. "What's this?" He reached into a patch of ivy and pulled something out. He held it in the air for her to see. A barrel key.

Marie's pulse fluttered. "Any ideas where it's from?"

Brandon shrugged and held it up higher to catch the landscape lighting. The key carried the patina of age and had a leaf-shaped end. "There are a few of the old doors in the house that use a key like this, but this looks like the wrong size."

"Where else could it have come from?"

"Lexie Thornton had a crew here working on the garden. Maybe it belongs to one of them."

Of course. Lexie had designed the garden. Her family's landscaping company had provided all the plants, the fountain and the bench. "Maybe Lexie could tell us more, not just about the key. Maybe she can help point us to whatever it is we're looking for."

"How late is too late to give her a call?" Brandon glanced down at his watch.

"I don't know. She works so hard, I'd hate to wake her. Maybe we should look around a little more first, try some of the doors in the house."

"Sure. I'll ask Shelley if she knows anything about the key, if she's still here."

"And Isabella?" Marie couldn't help thinking the key had to be related to something that had been going on. And Isabella seemed to be hiding the most secrets of anyone at Drake House.

Brandon nodded. "Right."

They pushed up from the bench at the same time.

Beneath them, the concrete shifted. Brandon grabbed Marie's arm, steadying them both.

"What was that?" Marie said.

Brandon gripped the top of the bench and pushed. It moved under his hand.

For a split second, Marie thought she saw a hollow space in the base of the bench. A space with something that looked like paper tucked inside. "Wait. Do that again."

Brandon lifted the edge of the bench.

Marie leaned close, her pulse racing. This had to be it. She peered into the dark space. "The legs of the bench are hollow. And there's something…" She dipped her hand inside. Her fingers touched the edge of a rolled piece of paper. She pulled it out.

Brandon lowered the bench's seat back into place. "What is it?"

Marie unrolled the paper. At first she wasn't sure. All she could see were penciled lines. "This is strange. It looks like a drawing of some sort."

Brandon studied it over her shoulder. He guided her hand, positioning the paper to take advantage of the landscape lighting. "It looks like a diagram. A sketch of the undercarriage of a car."

Sure enough. She could make out the wheels and the axles, the engine area and the gas tank. "What is this?" She indicated a pointy object near the gas tank.

"Some sort of spike?" He raised dark eyes to meet Marie's. "It's positioned to puncture the gas tank."

A pop split the air and echoed off Drake House.

Marie's heart jumped. "What was that?"

Brandon stiffened. He spun around, looking for the source of the sound.

Another pop. The bench made a snapping sound and something hit Marie in the leg.

"Get down!" Brandon threw his arms around her. His body slammed into her, and both of them tumbled to the ground.

Chapter Thirteen

Brandon could feel the air rush out of Marie's lungs as he came down on top of her. He raised himself up on his elbows, trying to lift his weight off her. "Marie, are you okay? Say something." He held his breath, willing her to speak, to be all right.

She coughed, gasped, nodded her head. Her breath sputtered and caught. Scooping air into her lungs, she looked at him with wide eyes. "I'm fine. I'm... What *was* that?"

"A gun."

"Someone is shooting at us?"

"Yes." And Brandon had to get Marie out of here. He had to get her someplace safe. "Can you move?"

"I don't know. I think something hit my leg."

A bullet? Brandon's gut tensed. Had Marie been shot? "Where?"

She moved her left leg under him. "I can't... You'll have to get up."

"Not until you're out of the line of fire." Marie might already be shot. He wasn't going to move aside and risk her being hit again. "Move to the other side of the bench. I'll shield you."

"But you—"

"No arguments." He glared directly into her eyes. She had to listen to him. She had to do what he said. "Go."

She gave a nod.

He lifted his weight off her, balancing on hands and toes, as if he were doing a push-up.

Marie rolled in one place until she lay on her stomach. She started crawling.

Pain screamed up Brandon's damaged leg. Gritting his teeth, he held on, trying to compensate with his good leg and arms.

She moved out from under him. As she cleared his body, he could smell blood. Something dark glistened on one leg of her jeans.

Damn. He hadn't been fast enough. It had taken too long for him to recognize the popping sound, to realize what it was. And his failure had left Marie hurt. Shot.

Reaching the corner of the bench, Marie rose to hands and knees. She moved faster, slipping between the holly bush and the bench.

Another pop echoed off the house. Something hit the concrete bench close to Marie's head. Too close.

"Get down!" Brandon yelled. He struggled to his knees. To his feet.

"Brandon!" Marie screamed. She popped up behind the bench, as if she was going to jump out and save him. "You'll be shot!"

"Stay there."

Another shot cracked in his ear. Again, something hit the bench. The bench. Not him. Even though he was standing in plain view. Even though he was a big, open target. Even though he'd done everything he could think of to draw the fire to him and away from Marie.

"Marie, stay down." He raced for the bench. He climbed into a spot next to her. He brought his hand down on her head, physically pushing her head lower, under the protection of the bench. He laid his chest on top of her and he wrapped his arms around her body.

She hunkered down, making room for him. She trembled all over.

Brandon held her tighter. Anger balled in his chest like a hard fist. Marie had almost been hit again. She'd almost died. No matter how careful he'd been, no matter how hard he'd tried to shield her, protect her, she'd come so close to losing her life he could hardly breathe. "Why didn't you get down? Why didn't you do what I said?"

She shuddered, as if letting out a silent sob. "I thought…I thought you were going to be killed."

He forced a breath into tight lungs. She didn't understand. In true Marie fashion, she'd thought only about saving him. Only about making sure he was safe. "Whoever is out there, he's not gunning for me."

She shook her head, as if she didn't want to believe the obvious.

It didn't matter. Not now. Now the only thing that meant a damn was getting Marie out of this mess. And the first thing he had to do was douse these lights.

He peered over the bench. His cane lay in the center of the path, its wood dark against the oyster shells. Too far to reach. Even if the shooter wasn't gunning for him, Brandon couldn't chance it. He didn't dare move that far from Marie.

He looked down at his feet. What he wouldn't give to be wearing hiking boots about now. Or a pair of the steel-toed work boots Doug Heller preferred. His Bruno

Maglis would have to do. Any luck and their sheer expense would make up for what they lacked in heft. Yeah, right.

Forcing his arms to release Marie, he slipped one shoe off.

"What are you doing?"

"Giving us some cover. Stay down." He slid between Marie and the prickly wall of holly. Using his hands and one foot, he pulled his body forward until he reached one of the landscape lights, a canister pointing up toward the siding of Drake House. Holding the shoe by its toe box, he brought the heel down hard against glass.

The lense protecting the light cracked but held.

He struck it again. And again.

Finally it shattered. One more blow and the light went dark.

He moved to the next light, the only one left that illuminated the bench area where they hid. He pulled back his shoe, ready to strike again.

A gunshot split the air.

Brandon ducked. His heart pounded; his breath rushed in his ears. He twisted back to check on Marie. She hadn't moved. "Marie?"

"I'm okay."

Had that bullet been meant for him? He didn't think so. The other shots had been fired close to Marie, too close. If the shooter had aimed at him this time, he should have been able to do a better job of hitting his target than that.

Unless he was just trying to scare Brandon. Trying to get him to abandon breaking the second light.

Hands clammy, he grasped the shoe and brought it down on the lens. Two more blows and the bulb was broken. The area was dark.

He scrambled back to Marie. The shells around the bench dug into his hands, his good knee. Now that the would-be killer had lost his spotlight, Marie was safer. But he still knew where she was hiding.

Brandon scanned the garden, searching for another spot to hide. But most of the garden was young, the plants still small. Only the holly and boxwood were left from the old east garden. Only they were large enough to conceal two adults. And only the bench could stop a bullet.

There was nowhere else to go.

Brandon looked down at the shoe still clutched in his hand. Maybe Marie and he didn't have to find a new hiding place. Maybe they only had to make the shooter think they had.

He dragged the shoe against the shells, making a shuffling sound. After several seconds of that, he flung it into a far section of the garden. Slipping off the second shoe, he flung that one as well.

Now to get back to Marie.

He moved slowly, careful to make no sound, careful to avoid rustling against the bushes. When he reached Marie, he slipped his arms around her as he had before. Lying flat behind the bench, he held her back tight to his chest. He brought his lips to her ear, her hair like silk against his cheek. "Shh."

She nodded. She didn't move. She barely seemed to breathe.

A minute passed. Two. It seemed like forever. Finally Brandon could hear the crunch of oyster shells underfoot.

He listened, struggling to hear the sound, to track it, over the beat of his own pulse, the hiss of his own breathing.

It came closer. Closer. It stopped.

Beneath him, Marie trembled. He could feel the rise and fall of her chest cease as she held her breath.

He wrapped her close, shielding her. If only he had a weapon. His cane. Even one of his shoes. Anything. He'd fight. But he'd used everything he could think of. Everything he had. And all that was left was to wait and see if it was enough.

A siren screamed from the direction of the highway.

The police. Thank God.

Footsteps crunched on shells. But this time going away, getting faint.

The siren drew closer. Red and blue light flashed from the other side of Drake House, radiating out from the corner of the east wing like an aurora during an eclipse.

Unless the gunman was an idiot, he had kept running and was long gone by now. Brandon closed his eyes and scooped in a deep breath of Marie's scent. He lay there for several seconds, soaking in the feel of her, the knowledge that she was safe.

Finally he forced his arms to release her. He forced his body to move away. Cold air filled the warmth where she'd been. His chest ached with it. It was all he could do to keep himself from gathering her against him again.

He looked at her, wanting to make sure she was okay. His gaze landed on her bloody jeans. "Let me see your leg."

She sat up. Grimacing, she pulled the leg of her jeans up to her knee. A red stain darkened her calf.

He moved to the side to get a better view of her wound. He could see a cut. He could see blood, but not as much blood as he'd expected.

"It's not too bad," Marie said. "I think it's just a cut. Maybe from a fragment of the bench."

She was probably right. In everyday life, the size of the cut and amount of blood would have horrified him. After all Marie had faced in the past few days, it seemed like nothing. She was alive, after all.

She was alive.

He could hear footsteps circling the house from either side, and low, official voices. The police. Josef must have called. Or Shelley.

"Whoever was shooting at us must think I found something. That I know something. That's why he's trying to kill me. To keep me quiet. Like he did my father."

Marie had voiced that theory before. And it made sense. But to Brandon, it didn't feel right. He'd been asking as many questions as Marie. He'd been with her, in her father's quarters, in Charlotte's study, in the garden fishing the sketch from the bench. So why didn't the shooter see him as a threat, too? Why wasn't the shooter just as eager to kill him?

The words Marie heard in the psychomanteum filtered through his mind. *All Brandon loves will die.* And who did he love? Who had he always loved?

Marie.

TO BRANDON'S RELIEF, it didn't take long for the police officers to secure the house and grounds and lead Brandon and Marie safely inside. A few minutes later, Chief Hammer joined them. Dressed in jeans with what little hair he had left plastered flat to one side of his head, he obviously hadn't been at the station this time. He'd no doubt been sleeping comfortably in his bed beside Mrs. Hammer. And although Brandon didn't have unshakable confidence in the Jenkins Cove Police Department or their leader, he was unspeakably glad they were here.

They'd saved Marie's life.

He answered the door himself, ushering the chief inside. "Thanks for coming personally, Chief. I know it's late."

"Not a problem. You know that, Brandon. It's a good thing your housekeeper called about the gunshots. I'm glad we were able to get here in time."

"Your men did a good job."

"Glad to hear it. They're good boys. I just had a word with Benson over by the carriage house before I came in."

Guilt jolted through Brandon with the force of an electric shock. He gripped his cane in both hands. He hadn't even thought to check on Josef. "My chauffeur. Is he all right?"

"Seems okay. Pretty scared. Poor guy was shaking."

Brandon would have to find a way to make it up to him. Extra vacation time. Trip to Florida. Something. Shelley, too. She'd kept her head and called the police. Interesting that the one employee he couldn't account for was the one he and Marie had the most reason to suspect. "You might want to send a car over to my maid's house. Isabella Faust."

"Why is that?"

"She's been acting a little strange lately. And I have reason to believe she might be out to get Marie."

"Marie? You're sure she was the target in this incident, too?"

"She was the target. Believe me, if whoever was

shooting that gun had wanted me dead, I wouldn't be talking to you now. He was gunning for Marie."

Brandon tried to read the chief's eyes. Hammer didn't like Marie, and he didn't believe much of what she said. He'd made that much clear. Maybe once she showed him the sketch they'd found, he'd reassess her theories.

Brandon sure had. At least he wanted to.

Hammer finally nodded. "All right. I'll have someone check up on Ms. Faust. Anyone else I should know about?"

Brandon thought for a moment. "Ned Perry, the developer."

Hammer nodded. "So he's been after you, too? I should have known. The man is a making a nuisance of himself. Badgering folks all around town to sell their waterfront."

"I think he and Isabella might be doing a little scheming to get their hands on Drake House."

"Scheming? How would shooting at Marie Leonard help them get Drake House?"

"Marie thinks they want to cover up something she has found."

"Marie thinks, eh?" The chief didn't look impressed. "And what do you think?"

Good damn question. Brandon shifted his feet on the thick oriental rug. He gripped the head of his cane. Marie's theory still didn't feel right to him. But what was the alternative? The words of a ghost? Words he hadn't even heard himself? "I'm with Marie."

The chief smiled in an unsuccessful attempt to cover up his skepticism. "All right, then. I'll hear Ms. Leonard out. Any more ideas about who might have declared target practice tonight?"

None that had panned out. "Come on in the kitchen. Marie's in there and she has something to show you. It might make everything more clear." At least Brandon could hope. He led Hammer through the halls, past the formal dining room and into the kitchen.

Marie and Shelley stood in the food preparation area, leaning on opposite countertops. Even though Brandon had helped Marie bandage her leg and had given her instructions to keep it elevated, she was back on her feet, probably still feeling too shaken to sit for long.

Hammer focused on Marie. The lines in his jowly face deepened with concern. "How is it you were involved in two life-threatening incidents in one day, Miss Leonard?"

Marie met his eyes. Her back stiffened just a little. "Not by choice, Chief."

"Brandon said you have something to show me?"

"I do." She pushed away from the counter and held out the rolled paper. "We found this hidden in the hollow base of a bench in the east garden. I think my father stashed it there."

The chief unfurled the roll. Plucking a pair of reading glasses out of his pocket, he slipped them on his pudgy nose and squinted down at the sketch. "A car?"

Shelley inched closer, craning her neck to see. She cradled a tea cup in her hands, a sweet scent wafting over the brim.

"The undercarriage of a car," Brandon said. "And look at the spike positioned by the gas tank."

Hammer frowned. "What is this supposed to be?"

"The evidence you wanted." Marie's voice was low but rang with conviction.

Brandon hoped Hammer would see it the same way.

The chief focused on Marie. "Evidence of what?"

Marie didn't miss a beat. "Charlotte Drake's murder."

A choked whimper came from Shelley's throat.

The chief held the paper at arm's length, as if suddenly afraid it would bite him. "Is this real?"

Marie's eyes flashed. Her hands tightened to fists by her sides. "You mean did I quickly draw it up?" she said sarcastically. "Of course it's real. It's just what I told you it is."

Brandon moved to Marie's side. He knew she was frustrated with her push and pull with the police. But if she wanted Hammer to look into the case, if she wanted him to switch the deaths from accidents to murders, if she wanted him to call in the state police to investigate, she had to be more diplomatic. He rested a hand on her arm.

She let out a pent-up breath. "I'm sorry, Chief. I've had a tough day."

"No offense taken, young lady. I'll take this back to the station and look into it along with the rest of the leads we find."

"No." Marie reached out to grasp the paper.

Hammer pulled it out of her range. "What do you mean, no?"

"I want to see your photos of the vehicle," Marie said. "The one Charlotte died in."

Brandon was aware of Shelley stepping closer behind him.

Hammer kept his eyes on Marie. He shook his head. "I'm sorry. I can't let you do that."

"Why not?"

"You aren't family. You don't own the car. You're not

part of the investigation. In short, I have no reason to show you anything."

Brandon took a deep breath. "Then maybe you can show me."

Marie whirled to glance up at him. Turning back to Hammer, she nodded. "You can't say Brandon doesn't have reason to look at the photos."

Hammer watched Brandon intently, as if trying to read his thoughts.

Strange. Brandon hadn't felt scrutinized like this by a police officer since he'd been caught drinking beer underage during his first year of college. A lifetime ago. He was more used to the chief of police handling his routine calls personally, not searching for the truth in his eyes.

Finally the chief nodded, as if he'd made up his mind about something. "There are no photos."

"No photos?" If it was possible for Marie's eyes to grow wider, they did. "What do you mean? Aren't they part of the accident report? Isn't taking pictures of a car involved in a fatal accident routine?"

"My officers must have overlooked it."

An uneasy feeling crept up the back of Brandon's neck. That could be true, except an officer hadn't overseen the accident report. As with most of the things involving the Drakes, Chief Hammer had hovered over the incident personally. And although Hammer had a reputation for being lazy, Brandon couldn't believe he was this lazy, not about something as serious as a death, accidental or not. "Why weren't pictures taken, Chief?"

Hammer looked down at the tile floor, the overhead lights reflecting off his scalp. "I thought…I thought it might get…inconvenient."

"Inconvenient?" Brandon parroted. "What in the hell does that mean?"

Hammer raised his eyes. "I don't think you want me to spell it out."

What was he getting at? Brandon had no clue. And he wasn't sure he wanted to know.

"You don't need pictures of her car," Shelley said.

All of them turned to look at the housekeeper.

She gripped her tea, her hands shaking so badly the steaming liquid sloshed over the edge of the cup and onto reddened fingers. She stared from Brandon to Marie, as if unaware she was burning herself. "The car itself. Her car. It's in a salvage yard outside town."

"It's still around?" The chief stared at Shelley as if she were speaking another language. "It was supposed to go to a crusher. It was supposed to be destroyed." He glanced at Brandon, his expression strangely apologetic.

"Shelley, are you sure it's still there?" Marie asked.

The woman nodded her gray head vigorously. "I see it every week."

"You must be mistaken." Again Hammer shot Brandon that strange look.

"I'm not mistaken. Believe me. I pay the rent, and Joey keeps it for me. Just like it was. I visit it every week. It helps me remember. Helps me keep her alive."

Brandon stared at his housekeeper. The woman visited the car in which Charlotte died? She paid someone to keep it for her? The idea was disturbing. Twisted.

Shelley's face crumpled. Tears rolled down her taut cheeks. "That paper, what does it say? What does it mean?"

Marie stepped toward Shelley. She laid a gentle hand on the woman's arm. "Charlotte didn't die in an accident, Shelley. I'm so sorry."

"What are you saying?"

"That paper and the car you've been caring for prove that Charlotte was murdered."

"Just a minute, Ms. Leonard," the chief boomed. "It doesn't prove any such thing."

"It will when we examine the car," Marie insisted. "We'll know then."

Shelley's tears gushed harder. The woman's wiry body convulsed in a sob. "Who could have done that?" She focused on Marie, and for a moment Brandon thought he saw a flash of hatred in her eyes.

"Calm down, Shelley," he commanded. "It wasn't Marie, for God's sake. But with your help, we can find out who did it. We're going to find out."

Shelley drew in a shuddering breath and nodded. Blindly she set her cup on the counter, then covered her face and softly cried.

Marie stepped beside her and placed a tender hand on the woman's shoulder. She said something soft in her ear, too quiet for Brandon to catch.

"I'm sorry," Shelley whispered. "So sorry." She reached for Marie, and Marie wrapped the woman in her arms.

Brandon looked back at Hammer. "I think you should call in the state police."

"You really want to do that?"

Brandon frowned. Strange. The chief's words sounded ominous, almost threatening, but his tone of voice was just plain worried. "Why wouldn't I?"

"You want it straight?" Hammer asked in a low voice.

Brandon answered with a nod.

"Because if your wife was murdered, the state's first suspect is going to be the husband, that's why."

Understanding rippled through Brandon. Suddenly it all made sense. The chief's hovering. His laziness in taking photos of Charlotte's car. Maybe even his reluctance to look at Edwin's death as anything but an accident. "You think *I* was responsible?"

Hammer waved off the words. "I don't think anything."

"You do. And you're protecting me."

Hammer didn't confirm or deny, he just held up the paper in his hand. "What do you want me to do with this? I'll handle it however you say."

Brandon shook his head. He'd never needed Chief Hammer's special protection. He'd never asked for it, never wanted it. And although he now realized it was merely part of his birthright, part of being a Drake in a town like Jenkins Cove, he felt a little sick at the double standard wealth gave him.

He looked Hammer straight in the eye. "Give the sketch to the state police. And while you're at it, call them right now and have someone meet us at the salvage yard owned by Shelley's friend. We have a car to examine."

Chapter Fourteen

The sun was starting to pink the eastern sky by the time Marie, Brandon and Chief Hammer met a Maryland state police detective named Randall McClellan at Joey Jansen's Auto Salvage east of Jenkins Cove on Route 43. Tucked into the base of a narrow neck of land clustered with vacation homes, the junkyard consisted of two corrugated buildings surrounded by rusted and twisted skeletons of cars and signs proclaiming Off-Season Boat Storage, Cheap Prices!

Joey, a man young enough to be Shelley's son and with a facial tick that looked to Marie as if he were constantly winking at her, led them to one of the steel sheds. He unlocked the door, apologized that there were no electric lights in the place, then announced he was going back to bed.

Marie let the men lead the way. A mixture of covered boats and a few pieces of farm machinery packed the large shed. The detective led them through the narrow paths between covered hulks with the flashlight he'd brought from his car. Finally his beam shone on a blackened and twisted steel skeleton against the back wall.

Charlotte's sports car.

Even though it had been six months since the fire, the stench of burned plastic and upholstery made Marie's eyes water as she stepped close. Oily and thick, the odor clogged her throat just as it had in the psycho-manteum. She could still hear the roar of the fire echoing through her memory.

Marie watched Brandon as he studied the car. Seeing the vehicle where Charlotte had died was hard enough for her. It had to be excruciating for him. Without thinking, she reached for his hand.

He squeezed her fingers and offered a tight-lipped grimace. "I'll look under the rear bumper, see if the spike is there."

His eyes looked tired, empty. Marie knew he was torturing himself by making himself face Charlotte's death all over again. But to what end? To punish himself for past mistakes? To reinforce the wall he'd built around his feelings for Marie? To give him the impetus to push her away again? She couldn't let him do it. Not now that they were so close to resolving this, so close to proving he had no reason for his crippling guilt.

She held his hand fast. "Let the detective look."

He held her gaze for a moment. And for that moment, time seemed to stop. Finally he nodded. "You're right. It's up to the police now, not us. Not anymore." He glanced at the detective and shifted to the side, giving him room to pass.

As if purposely unaware of their drama, Detective McClellan took one last look at the sketch they'd given him and moved to the car's rear. He crouched low and directed his beam under the back bumper, sweeping the undercarriage with light.

Marie forced herself to breathe. If the spike was no

longer attached to the car, she didn't know what she would do. She was out of leads and she was almost out of hope. Tonight, for the first time, the reality that someone wanted her dead had finally penetrated her thick skull. And worse, she understood that in protecting her, Brandon was in danger, too. She wanted to be done with this investigating stuff. She wanted the professionals to take over. She wanted the sketch to be out of her hands, and there be no more reason for fear.

But more than any yearning she had for safety, she wanted Brandon to know Charlotte hadn't killed herself. That for all his mistakes, all the mistakes everyone had made ten years ago, there was still a future for him and for her. Maybe even the promise of happiness.

Detective McClellan straightened, nearly as tall as Brandon himself. Marie searched his face for a clue of what he'd seen, but his flinty eyes were unreadable. He turned to Brandon. "We'll have to take the car."

"Fine with me."

"And I'd like to look around your property. And inside the house. I can have an evidence crew there this afternoon. Is that a problem, or should I call a judge?"

"You don't need a warrant. You'll have free run of the place."

A trill shimmered up Marie's spine. She wanted this so badly, she was afraid to speak, afraid to hope. But she had to know. She forced the words from her mouth. "Does this mean you'll look into Charlotte's and my father's deaths?"

Detective McClellan's mouth flattened to a line. "I have evidence sufficient to believe Charlotte Drake was murdered."

Relief warmed her like a double shot of brandy, making her feel light-headed and unsteady on her feet. "And my father?"

The detective peered down at her, his expression unchanging. "I'm sorry. Unless more evidence comes to light in your father's case, I have no reason to believe a crime was committed."

"I'LL HIRE A PRIVATE INVESTIGATOR. A professional. Someone good. He'll find the evidence the police need." Brandon watched Marie's face as Josef drove them back to Drake House. The morning sun had crept into the eastern sky, but even its warm rays couldn't dispel the darkness of the state police detective's pronouncement about Edwin's case.

Marie shook her head. "I'll keep looking. I still have some of his things to go through. I'm sure I'll find something… Something has to help."

She looked tired. Hurting. And Brandon didn't know what to do about it. He'd never felt so powerless in his life. "Now that the police believe Charlotte was murdered, it's only a matter of time. You know that, right? Edwin had to be the one who hid that sketch. He had to be killed because he knew who murdered Charlotte. When Detective McClellan finds who that is, he'll solve Edwin's murder as well."

"I know." She smiled up at him. "The important thing is that you know Charlotte didn't commit suicide. You know it wasn't your fault."

He let her words sink into him, let them circulate through his bloodstream, warming him to the core. But as good as it felt, he knew it wasn't that simple. Even though he knew Charlotte hadn't killed herself, he wasn't absolved of everything. "I made a lot of mistakes. I hurt Charlotte. I hurt you."

"You hurt yourself."

He nodded. But that wasn't important. Not as important as the burden of knowing he hurt people he cared for, people who cared for him. He looked down at his hands, suddenly aware he was twisting the wedding band on his finger.

He hadn't felt right about removing it when Charlotte died. He'd worn it like a penance. A constant reminder of what he'd done to her, the tragedy he'd caused. But now that he knew he hadn't caused that tragedy, it felt blasphemous to treat a wedding band as punishment. Somehow it felt disrespectful to Charlotte. To the wonderful woman she was.

He slipped it off.

Marie said nothing, but he could feel her watching. He could feel her body close and smell her delicious, spicy scent.

If only he'd trusted his feelings for her ten years ago. If only he'd stood up to what was expected of him and listened to his heart. He still would have hurt Charlotte, still would have been unfair to her. But her hurt would have faded, and she would have had a good life. Marie and he would have had a good life.

Despite the unease still niggling at the back of his mind, he'd like to believe they could have that good life now.

The car slowed and turned. Passing the redbrick and iron gate of the Manor at Drake Acres, it went through the simple white pillars announcing Drake House. Brandon pulled in a breath and peered out the window.

Black soot still stained the gray stone wall. A bouquet of flowers lay at the foot of the small cross Edwin had placed on the site. Flowers arranged by Shelley, no doubt, and placed with the utmost care. "Stop for a moment, Josef. Will you?"

The car slowed to a stop.

Brandon sat still, watching out the window. "I've never looked at that spot. Not since that night. Every time Josef drove me past, I averted my eyes. I just couldn't…"

"It's different now." Marie's voice sounded hushed, respectful and so wise.

"Yes. It looks different in the sun." He thought about placing the ring on the cross. Thought about bringing it to her grave outside Jenkins Cove Chapel. But in the end, he knew neither option felt right. He slipped it into his pocket. Charlotte was a part of him. A part of his past. And even though he would never again wear it, he would keep the symbol of their marriage with him. To remember the good things…and the mistakes.

"Go ahead, Josef."

The car resumed moving down the drive. He didn't remember getting out. Didn't remember walking to the house and unlocking the door. Didn't remember turning off the alarm and ensuring that the house was empty. All he remembered was taking Marie's hand in his and leading her upstairs.

He felt as though he'd waited ten years for this. He supposed he had. He peeled off her coat, her blouse. He pulled off her jeans tenderly over her bandaged leg and stripped her panties and bra.

The soft light of morning glowed through the bedroom window and kissed her skin.

When he'd last made love to Marie, she'd been a girl.

Now the naked body before him was that of a woman.
And he couldn't quite catch his breath. "You're beautiful."

She looked down at the floor.

He slipped his hand to her face and tilted her chin
up. "You're the most beautiful woman I've ever known."

He brought his mouth down on hers, tasting her,
savoring her. She kissed as she had in his dreams,
light and caring one moment, passionate and needy the
next. Smelling her scent aroused him. Touching her
filled him up.

She raised her hands to his shoulders, combed her
fingers through his hair. She moved one hand to his face
as they kissed, and traced her fingertips over his cheek.

The skin had once been so tender, so sensitive that a
whisper of air inspired agony. Back then, after the car
fire, he'd wished he couldn't feel anything. He'd prayed
for it. Now her touch felt faint, his nerve endings protected by scar tissue. And for the first time he wanted
to scrape it off, to dig deep, to feel.

For the first time he wanted more.

Without releasing her lips, he shucked his clothes. She
helped him, unbuttoning his shirt, pushing his pants down
his legs. He wanted to be as naked as she was. He wanted
to feel every inch of her skin with every inch of his.

When the last piece of clothing fell, he picked her
up in his arms and carried her the few steps to the bed.
It was an old-fashioned move. Something he'd seen in
the movies. Something he'd never thought a modern
man would do. But it felt fitting. It felt right.

He lowered her to the bed, gently, so gently. He
feathered kisses down her neck and over her collar-
bone. He worshiped her breasts with his mouth, his

tongue, his teeth. He'd never wanted another woman this way, only Marie. He'd never felt so powerful and strong and important as when he looked into her eyes.

He kissed her whole body. Her belly. Her thighs. Between her legs. And when shudder after shudder took her, it was the best feeling in the world.

When he kissed his way back to her mouth, she rolled him to his back and smiled. Moving down to his legs, she traced her tongue up the scars on his legs before devouring him with her warm, wet mouth.

She moved her lips up and down his length, stoking his want, drawing out his need. He felt as though he'd explode—with need, with love, with more happiness than he'd ever dared to dream. And when she came back to his lips, he took her mouth, tasting himself, tasting her, wanting more.

She sat up, arching her back. Sun caressed the curve of her breasts, lit her taut, reddened nipples. She moved over him and positioned him between her legs.

Sinking down, she accepted him inside.

He groaned as her slick heat enveloped him. Swallowed him. Claimed him. He covered her breasts with his hands, feeling her softness, reveling in her strength. He didn't know how long they moved like that, her on top, him on top, every way they could invent. Not long enough. Too long. It didn't really matter. Finally pleasure shuddered through her and spread to him as well. Release. Redemption. And when their bodies calmed and the sweat slicking their skin cooled, he cuddled her close. "I love you, Marie. I always have. More than I thought I could love anyone."

She smiled, a beautiful, open smile. "I love you, too, Brandon. And I'll never stop."

Her voice curled inside him. Her scent marked him. Her body melded to his. She was so precious to him, so perfect. He always wanted to hold her. Never wanted to lose her.

To lose her.

He pushed the thought away and snuggled a kiss into the crook of her neck.

Her giggle bubbled through him. Light. Carefree. Just what he wanted. To be carefree. To be untroubled. For once in his life to be happy.

But he wouldn't have those things. Not if something tragic happened. Not if he lost her.

His chest felt tight. His leg started to ache. He was being morose, but he couldn't help it. He had everything he wanted—right now, right here—yet he was more conscious than ever of how quickly it all could be taken away. How quickly Marie could be taken away.

All Brandon loves will die.

The words beat in the back of his mind like a war drum. Matching the beat of his heart. Overwhelming it. He didn't believe in ghosts. Not really. He'd never seen one, never heard one. Why would he believe a ghost's words?

He rolled his shoulders to loosen them. He tried to breathe deep, to draw in her scent, to pull oxygen into his starving lungs, but the pressure was too strong to shrug off. The fear was too strong to push away.

Maybe it wasn't about believing or ghosts or any of that. Maybe it was just about Marie. And if there was even the slightest chance that loving him was putting her in danger, it was a risk he couldn't take.

Chapter Fifteen

Marie didn't want to get out of bed. She didn't want to move away from Brandon. She didn't want to shower and wash off Brandon's scent from her skin. She felt if she disturbed this perfect moment, this perfect scene, the magic they had finally found might slip away.

Chimes rang through the house. The doorbell downstairs. She could hear the click of Isabella's footsteps crossing the marble foyer.

She flinched. "I don't want to move."

Brandon ruffled her hair with his fingers. "Can you see the surprise on Detective McClellan's and his evidence team's faces when they come up to search the master bedroom and find us naked in bed?" Brandon's words were light and joking, but something in his voice made Marie uneasy.

She propped up on an elbow and studied his face. "What's wrong?"

He shook his head, but he didn't meet her eyes.

"Please, tell me." Her voice sounded strained, frightened to her own ears. She *was* frightened. The way he'd avoided looking at her scared her to death.

She was probably overreacting. The last time she'd

made love with Brandon and let herself feel this happy, her whole world had come tumbling down around her. But things were different this time. Weren't they? There was no pending marriage. Their age difference didn't matter anymore. And after this morning's revelation, nothing was in their way. Everything had changed.

Brandon cupped the back of her head in his hand and pulled her snug against him.

Marie leaned her head against the solid strength of his shoulder. She knew there would be tough times ahead. She knew everything wouldn't be magically okay. That was fine. Brandon would never totally put the pain of the past behind him. Neither would she. But now that they had each other, maybe they could move forward. Bit by bit. Day by day. They could be happy together. At least after this morning, she dared to hope. "Whatever it is, you don't have to worry. We'll handle it. Together."

He didn't answer.

She could feel her heart rate rise, beating against his chest. Her throat grew dry. "Brandon?"

"You need to go back to Michigan."

His words jangled through her with the force of an electric shock. She sat up. As an afterthought, she pulled the sheet up, covering her breasts. "What do you mean, go back to Michigan?"

"You'll be safe there."

"I'll be safe here. The police—"

"Don't need your help."

"I wish that was true. But they wouldn't even have looked into this if we hadn't made them."

"But we did. And they are." He reached up and ran his fingers over her shoulder, down her arm. "It's up to the police now. Remember? You helped me see that. You helped me step away and go on with my life. Now let me help you."

"But I don't have to go back to Michigan for that. I'll look for teaching jobs in Baltimore or D.C. My life is here now."

He pushed himself up from the pillow. The soft glow of the afternoon sun lit his bare chest.

"Isn't my life here?" Panic clawed inside her. She struggled to remain still. To not grab him. Shake him. "Brandon?"

He thrust himself from the bed. He stepped to the chair and stood there, naked.

Marie scanned his face. His body. Her focus landed on the long scar marking his leg. Brandon had other scars, not so visible. Scars not totally healed.

"How can you send me away?" Her voice cracked. She sounded hysterical. She felt hysterical. This couldn't be happening. Not now that he knew Charlotte hadn't committed suicide. Not after they'd made love. Not after he'd told her he loved her. "We're supposed to be together. We're supposed to be happy. How can you ask me to leave?"

He grabbed a thick terry cloth robe from the back of the chair. He pulled it on and tied it at the waist, covering himself. "It's temporary. It's for your own protection. Once Detective McClellan finds out who killed Charlotte and your father, you can come back."

She shook her head. She knew what he was saying was smart. It was safe. It made sense. But logical or not, she had the feeling that once she left, what she and Brandon had found would be gone. That once she walked out of Drake House, she couldn't come back again. "I love you, Brandon. I don't want to lose you again."

"You won't lose me."

"If I leave, I will. I'll lose you. I know it. I don't want to leave."

"No, Marie. If you *don't* leave, I'm afraid *I'll* lose *you*."

A wave of cold swept through her and penetrated her bones. She clutched the sheet tighter against her breasts. "What? Why? The police have the sketch. It's out of my hands now."

He shook his head. He raked a hand through his hair. He seemed conflicted. Desperate. As tortured as when he'd believed he was the cause of Charlotte's death.

Now he was really frightening her. "What is it, Brandon? Tell me."

He met her eyes. "'All Brandon loves will die.'"

He didn't have to explain where the quote came from. She'd heard it with her own ears, and she'd never forget. "Did Charlotte speak to you?"

"No."

"Then what has changed since this morning?"

He stared at her as if he wasn't sure how to answer.

"You told me you loved me this morning," she said. "You made love to me. I thought you wanted us to be together."

"I did. I do."

"I told you what Charlotte's spirit said *days* ago."

He raked his hair again. "I know. I just didn't really understand what it meant until now."

Her throat felt tight. As if she could scream and scream and never get the pressure to loosen. "What does it mean, Brandon? What does it mean to *you*?"

"That I could lose you." He tested the belt of his robe, as if it wasn't tight enough, as if he'd felt it coming loose. "What if it isn't just about who killed Charlotte and your father? What if it isn't about you snooping around?"

"What are you trying to say?"

He splayed his hands out in front of him, begging for her to understand. "I've been investigating this, too. I've been asking questions. I even helped you find that damn sketch. But someone tried to throw *you* off the roof. They cut the brakes in *your* car. They shot at *you* alone, even though I was a much easier target."

"All that stuff is about covering up the murders."

"What if it isn't?"

"Are you saying you're afraid I'm a marked woman?"

"No. I'm saying what if by loving you, I've *made* you a marked woman?"

She shook her head. She was hoping things had changed. She was hoping the proof that Charlotte was murdered had taken away Brandon's guilt. Taken away his fear. But she'd failed to realize the fear wasn't really about Charlotte. Maybe it had never been. Maybe it was older than his marriage to Charlotte and his summer with Marie. Maybe it was something rooted deep in Brandon himself.

Tears filled her eyes, making the room blur. She turned away. "You're blaming yourself again. Just like you did with Charlotte. Just like you always do. What are you so afraid of?"

He was in front of her in two steps. He gripped her shoulders, turning her back toward him, forcing her to look into his eyes. "'All Brandon loves will die.' You said you heard Charlotte's spirit speak those words." His voice was hard, almost accusing.

"I did."

"Do you believe in ghosts, Marie? Because it seems like if you believe in ghosts, you should listen to the things they tell you. You should believe the words they say."

Her throat felt thick. Her heart ached with each beat. For him. For her. "Loss is part of life, Brandon."

He released her arms. Shaking his head, he limped to the fireplace and grabbed his cane.

Tears rolled down her cheeks, but she didn't push them away. She understood what he felt. Understood what he feared. "Last week when I talked to my father, our discussion was so ordinary. The snow in Michigan. His plans to visit me at Christmas. The box of ornaments he sent me from when I was a kid. I never guessed I wouldn't hear his voice again. And when he died, all I could think about was all the things I wanted to say that I can never say now. But you know what?"

"What?"

"It isn't about the things I didn't say. It's about the time we spent together. Like every ordinary minute of that conversation. That's the stuff that is life. That's the stuff that makes up love. And if you send me away, that's the stuff you and I will never have."

"I love you, Marie. How can I not protect you?"

"You can't protect me from everything."

He shook his head slowly, as if he could hardly summon the energy. "I can't accept that."

Tears clogged her throat, choked her words. "Everyone will die. It's just the way things are. We don't get to decide. But, Brandon, we do get to decide

how we live. Who we share our days and nights with.
Who we love."

He paused in front of the mantel, clutching his cane
in both hands, leaning on it as if he couldn't stand on
his own. "I'll book you a flight for tomorrow morning.
That should give you enough time to finish packing
your father's things."

MARIE TAPED THE LAST BOX of her father's papers and
wrote her address on the label. Shelley would mail the
papers, a few family heirlooms and a handful of photo
albums to her address in Michigan. His clothing, shoes
and most of his furniture would go to charity. And the
rooms themselves would finally belong to Shelley.

Marie didn't cry as she looked around the space. She
didn't have tears left. Not anymore. Ten years ago, when
she'd left this place, she'd thought her heart was per-
manently broken. Now Brandon had mended it this
morning only to shatter it again.

This time she knew it was unfixable.

Her father had been right. Brandon would never open
himself to love. If it wasn't his engagement to Charlotte
keeping them apart, he'd find something else. And he
had. The real issue. Fear.

Marie walked into the bedroom. It had taken her all
day, but the room was bare. Only her mostly packed
suitcase remained in the corner. The bedsheets and
spread were still tucked in neatly on the bed. Her flight
to Michigan left in the morning, which meant she'd be
sleeping at Drake House one last time.

Sleep. She almost laughed. There wasn't a chance
she'd be able to sleep. She might not have any cry left
in her, but her heart squeezed with each beat. Her ears

kept hearing Brandon's words over and over. Her mind searched for things she could have said or done to make this turn out differently.

Too bad those perfect words and deeds didn't exist.

Shaking her head, she sat on the edge of the bed. Even if she couldn't doze off, she might as well go through the motions. She had nothing else to do. Nothing else to pack. And she could stomach no more goodbyes.

She slipped off one boot, then the other and dropped them on the floor. One hit something, producing a metallic clink. What was that? Had she missed something? She shoved off the bed and peered under the white spread. A watch lay on the rug. One of her father's old pocket watches.

She plunked down on the floor and cradled the watch in her hands. When Jonathan Drake was alive, he'd given his butler a new pocket watch every Christmas, and her father treasured them, wearing a different one each day. The thought that she'd almost left one behind made her stomach twist.

What else might she have missed?

Sniffing back her tears, she flipped the edge of the bedspread back. Crouching on hands and knees, she scanned under the bed. Even though the rug seemed clean, her nose tickled with dust. The edge of a small notebook caught her eye. She grasped it and brought it into the light.

At first it seemed like nothing, just a pad of paper he might have jotted messages or to-do lists on. Then she saw the indentations left from pressing the pencil or pen on the sheet above.

Marie's heart jolted. She scrambled to her feet and

raced into the sitting room. She ripped open the box holding items from his desk and fished out a pencil. Rubbing the pencil back and forth lightly across the indentations in the notebook paper, she started to see the indentations take shape. A short, curved stem emerged on the page...a simple leaf...and finally the U-shaped petals of a tulip.

Identical to the image she'd seen in the psychomanteum mirror.

She squeezed her arms close against her sides to steady herself, to try to keep her hands from shaking. Her father had seen the image, too. He'd copied it. And there was more.

She rubbed the pencil over the other indentations on the notebook page. Numbers formed in her father's abrupt script. No, not numbers. Letters. A name.

JENKINS COVE CHAPEL CEMETERY.

The graveyard where her father was buried.

Chapter Sixteen

Brandon paced the third floor. His leg ached to high heaven, but he couldn't care less. He was doing the right thing. He was. Wasn't he?

He wished tomorrow morning was already here, that Marie was on the plane, that she was safe. Every second that ticked by made him more nervous. Every creak of the old house made him long to run downstairs to gather her into his arms. To protect her? Or to tell her he'd changed his mind? To beg her to stay with him forever?

He didn't know.

The distant sound of an engine hummed from the front of the house. What the hell?

He raced to the door of his sitting room and across the hall to his study. He pulled aside drapes covering the windows facing the forest and driveway at the front of the house. This was where he'd seen the fire that had taken Charlotte's life. A small orange glow through the trees at the stone wall. But he didn't see a fire now. He didn't see a crash.

He saw headlights shining down the drive, moving

away. And immediately he knew the car, even though it had only arrived from the rental agency the day before.

Where did Marie think she was going?

MARIE WRAPPED HER JACKET around her shoulders and quickened her steps up the redbrick path that wound between boxwood hedges. The gray stone church and walled graveyard were smack in the middle of town, right on Main Street. But that didn't seem to matter to her jumpy nerves.

A cemetery was still a cemetery.

She'd tried Sophie's breathing exercises. They didn't work. The only thing she could think of as she was scooping in those big, slow breaths was that she could hear sounds around her. Footsteps following up the path behind her. The creak of someone watching from the willow oaks overhead. Moans from among the gray, lichen-covered stones.

She had to reel in her imagination.

She pulled the notebook from her bag and tilted the page toward the light from the nearby street. Why had her father included both the sketch and the cemetery name on that page? She knew they were related. The two things were grouped too deliberately on the page not to be. Had he seen both the tulip and the name of the graveyard in the psychomanteum mirror? She'd seen the tulip right before Brandon had rushed into the room, responding to her scream. If she hadn't been interrupted, would Charlotte have shown her the rest?

Charlotte.

Charlotte was buried in this cemetery. Generations of Drakes were, as were many of their loyal servants who attended the chapel alongside the family. Would finding Charlotte's grave make the tulip's meaning clear? But how could she locate the grave in the darkness?

Maybe she should have roused Brandon and asked him to come with her. He would be able to lead her directly to Charlotte's headstone. And as painful as it would be to spend her last hours in Jenkins Cove with him after he'd pushed her away, at least she wouldn't be walking through graves alone.

No. He would never have let her come. Not as determined to protect her as he was. Once he made his decision, she knew he wouldn't let her go anywhere but to the airport. He would insist she turn the notebook over to the police. And they would file it away, never knowing what importance the drawing held.

Not that she knew, either. At least not yet.

She glanced around the perimeter of the yard. Just over the redbrick wall, she could hear a car's engine as it buzzed down the street. She could see the night-lights of the stores along Main Street. Some insomniac soul was burning the night oil in a nearby house.

She'd never been afraid to walk around Jenkins Cove by herself. No one was. Half the residents still didn't lock their doors, at least not during the off-season. She didn't need Brandon's protection. And she didn't need his help finding Charlotte's grave, either.

She could do it herself.

She reached an opening in the boxwood. She stepped off the path onto the sparse, winter grass. The dappled glow of nearby streetlights kissed the cemetery, filtered through thick, evergreen leaves of magnolia and wispy branches of willow oak. Tombstones of different shapes and sizes jutted from the ground like jagged teeth. They crowded every space between tree trunks and shrubs, some old as the town itself, some new...like her father's.

Marie hadn't noticed Charlotte's grave during her father's funeral, but then she'd been focusing on holding herself together and on the upcoming discussion she'd planned with Police Chief Hammer. It could be in the same area, and she'd simply missed it. At least she knew some Drakes were buried in that area. It was a place to start.

She wound through the stones, rubbing her arms to ward off the chill. If spirits roamed Drake House, surely they must roam this place. She thought she could feel them. The cold pockets of still air. The hair rising on the back of her neck. The soft beat in her ears that she swore had to be footsteps.

Or maybe the beat of a heart.

She shivered again, tamping down her imagination. She had to focus on the tulip. She had to find what it meant, what connection it had to the cemetery. She rounded a tree and spotted a white spire thrusting into the night.

The marker of Brandon's father, Jonathan Drake.

She remembered the tall column of stone, reminiscent of the Washington Memorial across the Chesapeake in the nation's capital. She couldn't help thinking of Brandon's uncle. When Clifford Drake died, no doubt his memorial would be twice as tall.

A twig cracked behind her.

She whirled around, but all she could see were stones, trees, shadows. She pushed out a tense breath and moved on. One by one, the Drake name started popping up on the headstones around her. Her father's grave was closer to the wall, deeper in the cemetery. But judging by the increased frequency of the Drake family graves, Charlotte's had to be close by.

She scanned each name. Mirabelle Drake, who died in 1933. Samuel Drake, who died as an infant twenty years earlier. William Drake, 1883, possibly one of the first Drakes buried in the yard.

Charlotte Drake.

Charlotte's stone was smooth. No mark of a tulip. No sign of the violence that had taken her life. Just beautiful, flawless, white.

Marie swallowed into an aching throat. She'd never liked Charlotte, but that wasn't due to anything Charlotte had done. It was because of what she had. It was because she was living the life Marie had dreamed of. It was because of jealousy and envy and bitter resentment.

Marie felt ashamed of those feelings now. She felt ashamed she'd been so hard on Brandon's wife. "I'm sorry, Charlotte. I'm sorry things worked out so badly for you. I'm sorry things worked out so badly for me. And most of all, I'm sorry Brandon will never know happiness."

The chill surrounding her faded and the air warmed. Marie blinked back the tears pooling in her eyes and scanned the stones around her. Maybe there was no tulip. Maybe Charlotte was the reason she had to come here tonight. To speak to her one last time. To put everything between them to rest.

Feeling less tense, Marie walked to her father's grave, the earth on top still rough and mounded. She'd felt Charlotte's presence in the graveyard, but she could tell right away her father wasn't there. His stone felt like just a stone. The mound of dirt covering his casket was just dirt. She pressed her lips together and studied the flowers clustered around his grave. "Goodbye, Daddy. Wherever you are. I'll miss you every day."

She turned away from the stone and wiped her eyes. She shed still more tears. A miracle. When her vision cleared, she focused on the brick wall. Concrete squares lined the length of the wall, vaults for cremated human remains. Each one held another name, another loved one who would never come back. The dates they died. The special bonds they had with family and friends and community.

And one held the simple etching of a tulip.

Marie sucked in a breath. She stumbled to the marker and fell to her knees.

She didn't have to compare the image to the one her father had drawn in the notebook. It had been burned into her brain in the psychomanteum. She read the name.

Lala Falat.

A foreign name. Maybe Eastern European.

The story Chelsea and Michael told her after her experience on the roof filtered through her mind. They'd said the doctor, Janecek, had smuggled people into the United States from Eastern Europe. He'd made them pay for their passage by donating their organs. Many had died. The state police were still counting the bodies.

Could Lala Falat be tied to the mass grave? And if so, what could she possibly have to do with Charlotte Drake? And why did her father think her grave was important?

Marie dug into her bag. Her hand closed over her digital camera. She pulled it out and focused the camera on the wall marker.

And the world went black.

"MARIE?" Brandon quickened his pace. He swore he'd heard the low whisper of her voice on this side of the graveyard. "Marie? Are you in here?"

Damn this leg. By the time he'd awakened Josef to drive him, Marie had a substantial head start. He wouldn't even have known where she'd gone if she hadn't parked her car right on Main Street in front of the Jenkins Cove Chapel.

He wound through the headstones, making his way to her father's marker. What on earth would make her so intent on visiting his grave that she had to drive here in the middle of the night? And what had possessed her to come here alone?

He knew the answer. Or at least he could guess. She'd assumed he would nix the idea in an effort to protect her.

And the worst thing was that she was probably right.

He reached Edwin's grave site.

No Marie.

He made his way to the brick wall. Maybe if he walked the perimeter, he could locate her.

His foot hit something in the grass.

He bent down and picked up a camera. And not five feet away lay Marie's purse.

His lungs constricted. His pulse thundered in his ears. She never would have dropped these things. Not unless she was forced to. Not unless she was attacked.

He spun and headed back to the dark, squared outlines of the boxwood hedges. He had to reach the car. He had to find Marie. "Josef!"

The chauffeur didn't answer. Or at least, Brandon didn't hear him. He couldn't hear anything above the roar of his breath and the beat of his heart. "Josef!"

He reached the boxwood. He could move faster on the path's hard, brick surface, but still not fast enough. He approached Main Street and strode through the church's gate.

Marie's second rental was still parked at the curb. The black shadow of his town car hulked behind it. A man stood behind the town car, raised the car's trunk.

"Josef?"

The man bent down and picked up a large object. Something wrapped in a blanket or a bag. The way he strained, Brandon could see it was heavy. The package seemed to move. The man dumped it in the trunk.

No. Not a package… A body.

Marie.

Josef slammed the trunk and looked up at Brandon.

Brandon raced for the car. Pain shot up his leg. He gritted this teeth and pushed faster.

The chauffeur jumped in the driver's seat. The engine hummed to life.

Brandon reached the curb. He slammed into the passenger door and grabbed at the door handle. But the car jolted into gear. It shot away from the curb, tires screeching.

The door swung open under Brandon's hand. He ran, trying to keep up, trying to jump inside. His legs faltered.

The door handle ripped from his grasp. He staggered and fell to his knees in the street.

The taillights faded into the distance.

Chapter Seventeen

She had to find a way out.

Marie pulled in the moist air of her own breath into her lungs. The bag he'd slipped over her head and shoulders clung tightly to her skin. Duct tape cut into her wrists and ankles. She fought the need to scream. It wouldn't do any good. Once he'd taped her hands and feet, he'd stuffed a gag into her mouth and secured it with more tape before replacing the bag. The gag wouldn't allow her to make much noise. Not enough for anyone to hear.

All she could do was thump her feet against the wall of the trunk, and even then she didn't have enough space to get power into her kick.

Josef.

She'd heard his voice when she'd kicked him. His accent. The strange language he spoke with a fluent tongue. She still couldn't believe he was doing this. She couldn't understand it. He'd seemed so meek, so courteous. Why would he want to hurt her? What had she ever done to him?

She could feel the car slow beneath her. She could feel it turn. More driving, over loose gravel this time. Around twists and bends. Finally the motion stopped.

A door slammed. Footsteps moved to the back of the car. The trunk lock clicked its release. Cool air rushed over Marie's sweat-slick skin. The crash of waves against rock whipped on the wind.

His rough hand gripped her arm. He pulled her to a sitting position, strong fingers bruising her flesh.

She didn't know what he planned to do, but she wasn't going to let him do it easily. She twisted her body, wrenching from his grasp. Flopping back down in the trunk, she lashed out with her feet.

She hit something solid.

A grunt broke from his lips, followed by swearing in that other language. He gripped her arm again. His fist crashed down on her neck and shoulder.

Breath shuddered from her lungs. For a moment, she couldn't think, couldn't move. Pain shuddered through her.

He lifted her from the trunk and slung her over his shoulder.

A whimper stuck in Marie's throat. She swallowed it back. She couldn't give in. She wouldn't.

She willed her mind to clear, willed the pain to fade. She wasn't strong enough to fight him. And trying wasn't going to get her anything but hurt…or killed. She had to be smarter. Had to strike when she could make it matter. *If* she could make it matter.

He walked on, her body swaying on his shoulder with each stride. The scent of water rode the wind along with the sound of the lapping waves. Then Josef stopped. She heard a lock rattle. Her body brushed against what felt like the jamb of a door. His heavy footfalls moved over what sounded like a marble floor.

Drake House.

She'd heard Brandon calling her name in the grave-yard, even though she couldn't answer loud enough for him to hear. He must still be at the chapel. Without Josef, without the car, he'd have no way to get back to Drake House. No way to help her until it was too late.

She had to find a way out of this on her own.

Stairs creaked. She could feel the sensation of moving upward. He was taking her upstairs. To do what? She tried to think, tried to stay calm. There had to be a way to escape. There had to.

"You kick again, I beat your head." His voice was low, dead, as if bled of any emotion, any humanity.

He lowered her down, letting her fall the last two feet to the parquet floor.

Oxygen rushed from her lungs. She tried to breathe, but took in dust. She coughed and sputtered.

He pulled her up to a sitting position and yanked the bag off her head. Without saying a word, he strode out of the room.

She blinked against the light. She didn't recognize the room at first, but the molding along the ceiling and the carved woodwork proved they were in Drake House. The room smelled dusty, as if it hadn't been used in a long time. She focused on the trees outside the uncov-ered window. The room was facing the south side of the house, away from the water. She blinked her eyes. Her vision cleared. Details came into focus. Animals circled the room, carved into the moldings. They rimmed the fireplace mantel. They had to be in the nursery.

Josef thunked back into the room. Rugs and paper and broken sticks of furniture overflowed his arms. He dropped them near the front bank of windows. He walked back out, returning with another armload, as if he was raiding whatever he could find and piling it in here.

As if he was building a bonfire.

Marie's throat constricted. She struggled to breathe around the gag. She had to think. Clearly she couldn't fight Josef. Not only was she tied, but he was twice as strong. She'd found that out the hard way. But maybe she could talk to him. Reason with him. Convince him that she was a person, too, that he couldn't just burn her like trash.

She offered a pleading look and made a noise deep in her throat, words impossible to squeeze past the rag jamming her mouth.

"You have something to say?"

She fought the urge to flinch from the harshness of his voice. Instead, she forced her head to nod.

He stepped beside her. Grabbing the duct tape, he ripped it from her lips.

Her skin burned. The room blurred with tears. She coughed, spitting the rag onto the floor. "Why are you doing this?"

He looked at her as if he didn't understand the question.

"I've never done anything to you," she said. "I never would."

"I am not doing this to you."

Marie stared at him. His words made no sense. "Of course you're doing it to me. You're hurting me right now."

He shook his head as if she were the one speaking gibberish. "I am doing it to him. Like he did to me. I am paying him back." As if that was all he needed to say, he turned and plodded from the room.

There was only one "him" Marie could think of, but

it didn't make sense. Why would Josef want to hurt Brandon? Nothing the chauffeur was saying or doing made sense. She twisted, looking around the room. She had to find a way out.

Her gaze landed on the old radiator along the wall. It was made of metal. Some pieces of it might even be sharp. It was her only chance.

She pushed herself across the floor, a combination of scooting on the wood and moving her legs like an inchworm. Reaching the radiator, she positioned her back against its warmth and felt the bottom edges with her hands.

Her fingers touched hard edges. Not exactly sharp, but if she had some time, if she could stall, she might be able to rub the tape enough to weaken it. She might be able to set herself free.

She just needed time.

Footsteps stomped in the hall, approaching. Josef bulled through the door, his arms filled with another load. More fuel for his bonfire.

He threw the armful on the pile and turned to stare at her. "You moved."

"I needed to lean against the wall. My back is sore." Marie didn't have to act. The muscles in her back were sore. And with her ankles taped, she had a hard time sitting in the middle of the floor with nothing to lean on.

Josef grunted. He started back to the door.

"Wait!"

He stopped and glared at her.

"You said you were doing this to someone else, not me. That you were paying him back. Who? Who are you paying back? Brandon?"

"Yes, Brandon."

"Why? What did Brandon ever do to you?"

A shadow of something passed over his brutal face. Anger. Sorrow. "He took away my Lala."

Lala? "The woman whose ashes are in the wall vault? She has the tulip on her marker?"

"Lala means tulip. She was my tulip. She and I were to be married. Now she is dead. Murdered."

The fiancée who died. Shelley and Brandon had both mentioned the woman, and how devastated Josef was when she died. "But I thought she was sick. Didn't she die in the hospital?"

"An infection. That's what they said. An infection from the surgery."

She couldn't follow. She knew Brandon provided health insurance to all his employees, just as his father had. She'd grown up on that insurance. So how could Josef blame Brandon for his fiancée's death? "I don't understand. It's not Brandon's fault she died."

He stared at her, his eyes hard, his boxer's nose red with the burst capillaries of a heavy drinker. A man who'd tried to forget. A man in pain. "It is his fault."

She kept rubbing the tape. The man looked as though he was rapidly reaching the end of his patience. She didn't have time to waste. "How?"

"He made her have the surgery." He walked from the room.

Now she was really lost. He wasn't making sense. Why would Brandon make anyone have surgery? Maybe Josef was suffering some kind of psychotic breakdown. Maybe Lala simply had a life-threatening illness and Brandon was there helping Josef through it. Maybe that's why Josef blamed his feelings of helplessness and frustration on Brandon.

She rubbed the tape, pressing it against the iron radiator as hard as she could. Moving it as fast as she could. It wasn't working. The tape was weakening a little, maybe, stretching a little. But it wasn't happening fast enough. She was running out of time.

She groped under the radiator again. There had to be a valve somewhere. Maybe that would give her the sharp edge she needed. She touched something circular, ridged like the serrated edge of a knife, but not as sharp. It would have to do.

The heavy footfalls returned. Josef carried an armful of gossamer draperies, something large and red underneath. He threw the drapes on the pile. Then she saw what else he carried. A fuel can. He twisted off the cover.

The sharp scent of gasoline assaulted Marie's senses. She had to delay him. She needed more time. "There's something I don't understand. Why would Brandon force Lala to have surgery?"

"She needed to pay." His voice growled low with anger. It shook with frustration. "She had no money. I had no money. She needed to pay, and I could not help her."

"She needed to pay what?"

"For coming to this country. She needed to pay. Dr. Janecek would not let her come without the surgery. Without giving something to pay for her passage. He would not let her come to me." A sob broke from his lips, deep and low and full of agony.

The pieces fell into place in Marie's mind. "The human trafficking? The mass grave? Lala was one of the people Janecek smuggled? He forced her to give him an organ to pay for smuggling her into the country?"

Josef made a keening sound low in his throat.

Marie's head hurt. She rubbed the tape harder. Faster. Even though she'd tied the pieces together, what Josef was saying still didn't make sense. "It was Janecek who did those things. It was him who forced Lala to have the surgery. It was him who caused the infection. Why do you keep saying it was Brandon?"

He splashed gasoline on the draperies and rugs. "The Drakes. Brandon and his uncle. I break his uncle's things. I try to make him pay. But he does not care about anything like I care for Lala. Brandon does."

She remembered overhearing Brandon talking to Chief Hammer about some vandalism at his uncle Cliff's. That was Josef? None of this made sense. Why would he target the Drakes? "I don't know about Cliff, but Brandon would never do anything to hurt you."

He shook his head. "He would. He did. I saw the ship. I was brought in, too. Before Lala."

"What ship?"

"A big ship. It said Drake right on the bow."

"The ship used for smuggling?"

"Yes."

"Are you sure?"

"I lost my Lala. I must live alone. I will have no children." He looked at the carved moldings at the top of the nursery walls. Tears wet his rough cheeks. "My life is dead, yet I must live on. Well, if I must, then Brandon Drake must, too. He will know how it feels."

The words she heard in the psychomanteum echoed in Marie's mind. *All Brandon loves will die.* Was Brandon right? Were the people who cared about him marked for death? All to serve Josef's need for revenge?

"Charlotte?" She felt the tape give. Not entirely, but

a little. Her hands trembled and burned. The odor of gasoline stung her eyes. She held Josef's gaze and pushed on. She had to know. "Did you weld the spike near the gas tank? Did you crash Charlotte's car into the wall?"

"Lala came here to marry me. He took my wife. He did not deserve one of his own."

"And my father?"

He stuffed his hands into his pockets and stared down at the floor. "I could not let him tell. I am sorry."

"And now me?"

"You most of all. He loves you like I loved Lala. I cannot let him have you."

"You'll never get away with this. The police will know you did this."

He brought his hands out of his pockets, something in his fist. He looked up at her, his eyes dead. "I am not trying to get away. I am going with you. I am going to be with Lala, where I belong." He struck the match and threw it in the pile.

Chapter Eighteen

Brandon noticed the orange glow in the sky before he could see the house. It pulsated beyond the twisted, bare branches of oak, sycamore and wisps of willow, radiating like the eerie light of a coming storm. He pushed the accelerator harder. The engine of Marie's little rental whined. Its tires jolted over dips in the long drive.

A curve in the drive rushed toward him. Gritting his teeth, he forced his leg to respond. He lifted his foot from the accelerator. Hot pain shot through his thigh and hip, pulsed up his spine. He jammed his left foot to the brake. The little car fishtailed around the turn. He steered into the slide. The car righted itself. Remembering to breathe, he hit the accelerator again.

He'd lost so much time rushing back into the graveyard and finding Marie's purse. Time he couldn't afford to give Josef. But at least he'd found her cell phone and the keys to her car. At least he could call for help. At least he had wheels to get back.

At first he hadn't been sure where the chauffeur would take Marie. Then it came to him. Drake House. He could have killed her in the graveyard. It would have been easier. Cleaner. But his focus wasn't simply on killing her. He wanted to kill her at Drake House. The place where he'd tried to kill her the other times. And where he'd chosen to kill Charlotte.

All Brandon loves will die.

The words were true, just as he'd feared. It was all about him. Not Charlotte. Not Edwin. Not Marie. Whatever Josef had against him was personal. He'd want to do it at Drake House. He'd want to bring it home to Brandon.

The only thing Brandon couldn't figure out was why.

He fishtailed around another bend in the tree-lined drive. The trunk of a sycamore rushed at him. The car door missed the tree by inches.

He stomped on the gas.

He'd been so damn stupid. So stupid. He'd pushed Marie away. He'd tried to make her leave. He'd told himself he was protecting her, shielding her from a killer. But all he'd done was leave her alone and vulnerable. And tonight he'd brought Josef straight to her.

He hadn't protected her at all.

The car broke from the trees. Nothing obscured the fire now. It licked from the front windows of the east wing. Black smoke gushed into the air and engulfed the balcony. It carried on the air and made him choke.

He couldn't be too late. He couldn't.

He stomped the brake and the car skidded to a stop. He shoved his way out the door. He pushed as fast as he could go, jabbing his cane into the ground, pulling his legs along.

He shoved the front door open. Smoke hung in the air, making the grand staircase appear dim and gray. The fire was in the east wing. He'd noticed from outside. The nursery.

He raced over the marble foyer. Clutching the banister, he half pulled himself, half ran to the top of the staircase.

The air grew hot. His eyes stung and watered. Smoke thickened, choking out oxygen, making it hard to see.

He groped through the dark hallways. Low. He had to get low to the floor. The smoke would be thinner there. He could breathe.

He crouched down. It was easier to breathe, but he still couldn't see. Tears streamed down his cheeks. His eyes felt as if they were burning out of his head. He groped the wall as a guide and crawled.

He hoped to God Marie wasn't in the nursery. The way the flames were leaping from the front windows, if she was in that room, she was likely dead.

He couldn't believe that. He wouldn't.

A loud thunk shook the house. A cough rose above the crackle and hiss of fire.

A woman's cough.

Not from the nursery. It came from down the hall. He could swear it.

He crawled faster. His leg screamed with pain, but he didn't care. If he didn't find Marie, if he didn't reach her in time, he didn't care about anything. Not his leg, not getting out of Drake House, not living until tomorrow.

UNABLE TO REMOVE THE TAPE that bound them, Marie dragged her useless legs down the hall. She didn't know where Josef was. Didn't even know if he was alive or swallowed by fire. She'd made her move when he'd thrown the match. Adrenaline, survival instinct, what it was she didn't know. But when the fire flared, sucking the oxygen from the room and imploding glass from the windows, she'd finally ripped the tape free. She'd pulled herself out of the room and down the hall. She'd gotten away.

And she'd taken a wrong turn.

Unthinkingly she'd turned down the hall, racing away from the fire instead of turning back for the staircase. And now she had to find her way back to one of the staircases before she was trapped.

Smoke billowed around her, enfolding her in its gray darkness. She was all turned around. She couldn't see, could hardly breathe.

"Marie!"

She gasped and coughed. How had he gotten here? How had he reached her? Tears ran from her eyes, but not from the smoke. "Brandon! I'm here!"

"Move toward my voice. Stay low."

As if she had a choice. She scooched on her stomach, dragging her legs behind. Along the hall, back toward the heat, the fire. *Toward Brandon.*

A shape came out of the smoke. Brandon? Was he here?

Something smacked the side of her head. Hard.

She slumped forward, her eyes blurring, her ears ringing.

"Marie? Are you okay? What happened?"

No. Josef was here. Josef had found her. And now he would find Brandon. He'd hurt him. He'd kill him. "Brandon! It's Josef! It's—"

Another blow hit her and she couldn't say anything more.

Chapter Nineteen

Brandon could see shapes through the smoke. One crouching, like him. One lying flat on the floor.

Marie.

Growling deep in his throat, he launched himself at the larger hulk. He lashed out with his cane.

The blow connected. Its force shuddered up the teak and into the handle. A masculine grunt rose above the din of the fire.

Brandon swung again, fighting his way forward to Marie.

Josef moved back.

Brandon swung again. This time he missed, his cane whooshing through nothing but smoky air.

Josef slipped around the side of the hall. He circled around behind Brandon.

No.

He couldn't let Josef cut them off from the stairs. The man had a death wish. He must. He never would have stayed in the fire if he hadn't intended to die along with Marie. He would do everything in his power to keep them from escaping. And now that he was between Marie and closest the staircase, he might succeed.

Unless Brandon stopped him.

Brandon struggled to his feet. Swinging the cane in front of him, he crouched low, following Josef down the hall, pushing him back. They reached the nursery door. The heat was intolerable, fiery as a blast oven. The smoke gushed out into the hall, too thick to see through despite the blinding light of the flames behind Josef and the blown-out windows all along the front of the wing.

Brandon's muscles ached, but he kept swinging. "Marie! Get out! If you can hear me, get out now!"

Josef backed up under Brandon's assault, retreating into the nursery.

No, not retreating. He darted to the side and grabbed something from the room. Something long. He swung it at Brandon.

Pain slammed into Brandon's thigh. He blinked back the agony.

The gray shape he knew was Josef drew back its weapon, angling to land another blow. Even though the thick cloud, Brandon could see it was a stick of some sort. A broken piece of furniture.

Josef swung again.

Brandon blocked the blow with his cane. He jumped back, out of the doorway. His leg crumpled under him and he fell to the floor.

A larger crash rumbled through Brandon's head, through the whole of Drake House. The orange flames leaped. The nursery's ceiling closed down on them, falling, crashing. A flaming piece of molding landed on Josef, pinning him to the floor.

His scream ripped through the roar of fire, deep, guttural, full of agony. Flame jumped around him. Heat sucked air from the room.

Brandon scurried back. He couldn't help Josef. But he could still save Marie.

Or die trying.

The fire was hot. So hot. Smoke clogged his throat. Sweat dripped in his eyes.

He closed his eyes and felt his way along the hall back to the spot where he'd left Marie. The trek seemed to take forever. His hands touched nothing but smooth floor and wall moldings. The heat seemed to close in behind him.

His fingers brushed something soft. Silky strands of hair. He ran his hands over her, gripping the wool of her coat.

She stirred.

She was alive. Still alive. "Marie? Can you move? I need to get you out of here."

She made a sound, but he couldn't decipher words. She struggled to her elbows. "Feet."

He ran his hands down her legs. Duct tape affixed her ankles. He couldn't get it off, not without scissors or a knife to cut it. He'd have to carry her. "I got you. I'm going to lift you to my shoulder. I need you to hang on. Can you do that?"

He felt her nod.

He hefted her to one shoulder. She helped him shift her body into a fireman's carry position, slung over his shoulders and behind his neck. She locked her hands around his left arm. He threaded his right between her bound legs. They had to move.

Slowly, too slowly, he crawled down the hall. The nursery was engulfed in flame now, the air in the hallway too thick to breathe, the heat too intense to slow down.

Josef's screams had stopped.

Brandon pushed the chauffeur from his mind. He had to focus. He had to get Marie and himself out, or they would suffer the same fate as Josef.

He made his way down the staircase, half stumbling, half falling. He forced his feet to carry them across the marble foyer. He pushed his way outside.

Sirens screamed from the highway.

Brandon staggered to the lawn and fell to his knees. He released Marie's legs and lowered her to the cool grass.

She looked up at him, her face streaked with soot and tears. Her eyes red and swollen. Bruises bloomed on her delicate cheek. "Josef?"

"Dead."

She swallowed, flinching as if the action was painful. Her throat must be as swollen from the smoke as his. No, more swollen since she had breathed it longer.

"Police are on their way. Probably fire, too. Paramedics."

"I'm okay."

"No, you're not. Me, either. But we will be."

"You were right. Josef was trying to destroy everything you love. Charlotte, my father, me, Drake House." Her voice sounded choked. She swallowed hard and went on. "His fiancée was one of the people Dr. Janecek smuggled into the country. She died from an infection after the surgery."

It was a sad story. A tragic story. But it didn't explain a thing. "What does all that have to do with me?"

"He said she was smuggled into the country aboard a Drake ship."

"Drake Enterprises? A cargo ship or the yacht?"

She moved one shoulder as if trying to shrug. Flinching from pain, she aborted the move. "He said the name *Drake* was on the bow."

"Damn. I'll have to talk to Cliff about that. And Detective McClellan."

"Josef tried to hurt Cliff, too. The vandalism."

He nodded. The surest way to hurt Cliff was to destroy his toys. And the surest way to hurt Brandon was...

He felt sick. His throat ached, not just from the smoke. "I brought him right to you. He wouldn't have even known you were at the chapel graveyard except I asked him to drive me there."

Marie reached a hand to him. She traced her fingers over his face, his cheek, his scar. "It's not your fault. You couldn't have known."

"Maybe not about Josef, but I should have known enough to keep you by my side. To never let you go." He hadn't let himself think of it. Not since he'd seen her purse on the cemetery lawn. But he knew that was his mistake. That had been his mistake all along. "I've wanted you so long, Marie, that once I had you in my arms again, all I could think about was losing you. I couldn't let myself believe we could be together. It just felt too..."

"Fragile."

He nodded. And *he'd* felt fragile. Raw. Exposed. Vulnerable. "I didn't see until I lost you. I didn't understand until..."

"It's okay."

He shook his head. He had to explain this. He had to

make her see. "When I lost you, all I could think about was how I threw my chance away. Again. Our chance to be together."

Police cars flew into the clearing and screeched to stops in the yard. Another siren screamed up the drive. Lights flashed red against the bare trees. A fire truck barreled toward the house. Another screamed out at the highway.

He looked back to Marie. He had to finish. He had to make her see that he understood. He needed to know if she could forgive him. If she could trust him again. If she could love him. "I get it now. I understand. I can't protect myself from losing you. If you're here or in Michigan or halfway around the world, it's going to feel the same. It's going to destroy me."

Tears streamed down her face and sparkled in the fire's radiant glow. "You're not going to lose me, Brandon. I'm here. I love you. And I'm not going anywhere."

They were the most beautiful words he'd ever heard, and he soaked them up and held them in his heart. "I want to spend the rest of my ordinary moments loving you, Marie."

"Oh, Brandon. I—"

He hovered a finger over her lips. "Let me talk. I need to say this." It might not be poetic. He was sure it wouldn't be. But he had to say it. And he needed her to hear.

She nodded.

"I want all that stuff you were talking about. All that ordinary stuff, every day for the rest of our lives." He swallowed into a burning throat. "However long that will be."

A smile curved her lips. "It will be long, Brandon.

We'll have children and they'll have their own children. We'll grow old together."

More beautiful words. And looking into her eyes, he believed them. He knew from now on, he always would.

MARIE WATCHED LEXIE'S WORKERS bustle into the ballroom, hauling armfuls of the most luxurious poinsettias she'd ever seen, the first step in getting the room ready for the Drake Foundation's Christmas Ball. She was so glad they were going through with the ball. It seemed right. A fitting tribute to her father and to Charlotte. And a sign of the life and vibrancy she and Brandon intended to bring back to Drake House.

The cleaning crews had been amazing. She could barely smell the smoke from the east wing fire. And Lexie's plan of filling the room with pots of flowers to add more freshness to the air should take care of the problem nicely.

Even Isabella and Shelley had pitched in long hours without complaint. And although Marie was still a little guarded around the two of them, she felt they'd reached some kind of truce. Shelley had even warmed to her after their talk in the kitchen that night. Isabella had focused her romantic ambitions fully on Brandon's uncle Cliff. And even though Ned Perry was still out there buying up land for condos, the fact that he wasn't killing people to get it made Marie feel a lot more charitable toward him as well.

It was the season for giving, after all.

And now it was the season for deciding what she thought of Lexie's new ideas for decorating the ballroom before her friend came down from the balcony and demanded her verdict. But try as she might, she was having a heck of a time looking around the ballroom and making the sketches Lexie had shown her come to life in her mind's eye.

Marie tilted her head to the side, despite the residual soreness in her neck, and studied the mantle of the ballroom's grand fireplace. She just didn't have the talent for design that her friend had. Or the good taste of her father, for that matter. Although Lexie had explained her plans for garlands around the glass doors, a evergreen swag and candles on the fireplace mantel and a lighting effect that would look like snow falling from the sky, Marie couldn't see it. And she didn't want to let her friend down.

Brandon walked up beside her and slipped an arm around her shoulder. "What is it?"

"Lexie wants to know what I think of her plans."

"So what do you think?"

"I don't know. She knows this stuff better than I do. I wish she wouldn't ask me. I trust whatever she decides will look great."

"Then tell her that."

"I tried. She said she always ran things by my father. She wants my opinion."

"Tell her it will look beautiful."

"Unless I can really imagine it, she'll know I'm just saying the words."

"I think it's beautiful. In fact, I think it's absolutely perfect." But he wasn't looking at the mantel or the mirror above. He was staring straight at her.

She backhanded him in the ribs.

"Ow."

"Yeah, that hurt. Sure."

"Okay. It didn't hurt. But I like tickling better. Or kissing."

She let out a sigh. She couldn't help but smile. After all they'd been through, they'd finally found a way to be together. To share their love. To live their lives. Every ordinary minute they had left. "I'm happy."

"Are you?" Brandon gave her a grin. "I'm glad. I'm happy, too."

"I only wish…"

"What?"

"That my father was here. That he could see Lexie's plans. That he could let us know what he thinks."

Brandon's grin softened. He rubbed her arm gently with his fingertips. "You want his approval."

"Yes."

"You're not just talking about the Christmas decorations, are you?"

A tingling sensation stole over her. "No. I guess I'm not."

He leaned down and kissed her, light and gentle, a confirmation of their love and a promise of more love to come. "I have something for you." He took her left hand in his and slipped something onto her finger.

Marie held her breath. She lifted her hand and studied the ring.

It was a marquis solitaire diamond on a platinum band, sleek, classic, beautiful. And bigger than any diamond she'd ever seen. Not his mother's ring, but a new one. A fresh one. A ring just for her. "I love it."

He leaned on his cane. He grimaced as he lowered himself to a knee. "To make it official, you know."

Her throat felt thick. "I would love to marry you."

He shook his head. "You have to wait until I ask."

"Then ask, already." She couldn't help being impatient. She'd waited ten years for this. But the ten years had been worth it to see his smile now. To feel his unreserved happiness. To bask in happiness of her own.

"I love you, Marie Leonard. And I would be honored and humbled if you would agree to be my wife."

Marie smiled and nodded, unsure her voice would work.

He crooked his eyebrows. "Is that a yes? Because my leg is killing me."

She gripped his arm and pulled him to his feet. "It's a yes. Always and forever a yes."

He gave her a peck on the lips and glanced around the ballroom, watching the workers carry in another round of colorful plants. "I think Edwin would be happy. I think he would heartily approve." He kissed her, longer this time, deeper, and when he finished, he held her close against his side.

Marie's eyes misted. They had wonderful days ahead, wonderful years. And with luck, children to fill the new nursery that would rise from the old nursery's ashes. Rebuilt with detail and care to match the rest of Drake House.

She blinked back the tears and looked into the mirror above the mantel. Suddenly Lexie's decorating plans came alive in her imagination. Greenery draped on the mantel. Candles of different heights rose gracefully, their flames reflected in the glass. Light drifted through the ballroom like floating flakes of snow. Perfect.

And deep in the mirror's antique silvered glass, as real as her happiness, she could see her father's smile.

* * * * *

*There's nothing like
A Holiday Mystery at Jenkins Cove!
Don't miss the deliciously chilling and deeply
romantic conclusion to this trilogy.
CHRISTMAS DELIVERY
by Patricia Rosemoor
On sale December 2008 from Harlequin Intrigue.*

Here is a sneak preview of
A STONE CREEK CHRISTMAS,
the latest in Linda Lael Miller's acclaimed
McKETTRICK *series.*

A lonely horse brought vet Olivia O'Ballivan
to Tanner Quinn's farm, but it's the rancher's love
that might cause her to stay.
A STONE CREEK CHRISTMAS
Available December 2008
from Silhouette Special Edition.

Tanner heard the rig roll in around sunset. Smiling, he wandered to the window. Watched as Olivia O'Ballivan climbed out of her Suburban, flung one defiant glance toward the house and started for the barn, the golden retriever trotting along behind her.

Taking his coat and hat down from the peg next to the back door, he put them on and went outside. He was used to being alone, even liked it, but keeping company with Doc O'Ballivan, bristly though she sometimes was, would provide a welcome diversion.

He gave her time to reach the horse Butterpie's stall, then walked into the barn.

The golden retriever came to greet him, all wagging tail and melting brown eyes, and he bent to stroke her soft, sturdy back. "Hey, there, dog," he said.

Sure enough, Olivia was in the stall, brushing But-

terpie down and talking to her in a soft, soothing voice
that touched something private inside Tanner and made
him want to turn on one heel and beat it back to the
house.

He'd be damned if he'd do it, though.

This was *his* ranch, *his* barn. Well-intentioned as she
was, *Olivia* was the trespasser here, not him.

"She's still very upset," Olivia told him, without
turning to look at him or slowing down with the brush.

Shiloh, always an easy horse to get along with, stood
contentedly in his own stall, munching away on the
feed Tanner had given him earlier. Butterpie, he noted,
hadn't touched her supper as far as he could tell.

"Do you know anything at all about horses, Mr.
Quinn?" Olivia asked.

He leaned against the stall door, the way he had the
day before, and grinned. He'd practically been raised
on horseback; he and Tessa had grown up on their
grandmother's farm in the Texas hill country, after their
folks divorced and went their separate ways, both of
them too busy to bother with a couple of kids. "A few
things," he said. "And I mean to call you Olivia, so you
might as well return the favor and address me by my
first name."

He watched as she took that in, dealt with it, decided
on an approach. He'd have to wait and see what that
turned out to be, but he didn't mind. It was a pleasure
just watching Olivia O'Ballivan grooming a horse.

"All right, *Tanner*," she said. "This barn is a disgrace.
When are you going to have the roof fixed? If it snows
again, the hay will get wet and probably mold…"

He chuckled, shifted a little. He'd have a crew out
there the following Monday morning to replace the roof

and shore up the walls—he'd made the arrangements over a week before—but he felt no particular compunction to explain that. He was enjoying her ire too much; it made her color rise and her hair fly when she turned her head, and the faster breathing made her perfect breasts go up and down in an enticing rhythm. "What makes you so sure I'm a greenhorn?" he asked mildly, still leaning on the gate.

At last she looked straight at him, but she didn't move from Butterpie's side. "Your hat, your boots—that fancy red truck you drive. I'll bet it's customized."

Tanner grinned. Adjusted his hat. "Are you telling me real cowboys don't drive red trucks?"

"There are lots of trucks around here," she said. "Some of them are red, and some of them are new. And *all* of them are splattered with mud or manure or both."

"Maybe I ought to put in a car wash, then," he teased. "Sounds like there's a market for one. Might be a good investment."

She softened, though not significantly, and spared him a cautious half smile, full of questions she probably wouldn't ask. "There's a good car wash in Indian Rock," she informed him. "People go there. It's only forty miles."

"Oh," he said with just a hint of mockery. "*Only* forty miles. Well, then. Guess I'd better dirty up my truck if I want to be taken seriously in these here parts. Scuff up my boots a bit, too, and maybe stomp on my hat a couple of times."

Her cheeks went a fetching shade of pink. "You are twisting what I said," she told him, brushing Butterpie again, her touch gentle but sure. "I meant..."

Tanner envied that little horse. Wished he had a furry hide, so he'd need brushing, too.

"You *meant* that I'm not a real cowboy," he said.
"And you could be right. I've spent a lot of time on construction sites over the last few years, or in meetings where a hat and boots wouldn't be appropriate. Instead of digging out my old gear, once I decided to take this job, I just bought new."

"I bet you don't even *have* any old gear," she challenged, but she was smiling, albeit cautiously, as though she might withdraw into a disapproving frown at any second.

He took off his hat, extended it to her. "Here," he teased. "Rub that around in the muck until it suits you."

She laughed, and the sound—well, it caused a powerful and wholly unexpected shift inside him. Scared the hell out of him and, paradoxically, made him yearn to hear it again.

* * * * *

*Discover how this rugged rancher's wanderlust
is tamed in time for a merry Christmas, in
A STONE CREEK CHRISTMAS.
In stores December 2008.*